They stood and stared at each other for a long moment, the air around them starting to crackle with electric tension.

It had always been this way—ever since that first kiss so very long ago. Arthur glanced at her mouth…that perfectly sculptured mouth which had always fitted so perfectly with his own. Swallowing, he met her eyes, and only now that they were in the artificially lit kitchen did he realise she'd removed the contacts.

Bright blue eyes the colour of the sky on a cloudless summer's day gazed back at him, repressed desire visible in their depths. Maybelle bit her lower lip and he realised she was nervous. He didn't blame her. He was nervous, too. He knew it was possible for the physical attraction he'd felt all those years ago to return with a forceful thump, but the emotional connection—the one which their years apart should have wrecked—was also still very much alive.

Then, before he could think anything else, she r……………

wrap…………………………ed his r…

Dear Reader,

The world is full of trials and tribulations—and if you're a *Star Trek* fan, like me, sometimes it's full of Tribbles… But I digress. There are times when it feels as if the world is throwing curveball after curveball in our direction. But although we get knocked down again and again it's the getting up part which is the most important.

Throughout the many versions of this story I found a new level of normality—especially after the death of my beloved father, moving house and having my marriage end. There are so many of those curveballs we just don't see coming, and when they all come at once it can be very difficult to remain standing! That's when it's vitally important to reach out for those you can rely on.

Maybelle Freebourne and I went through a lot of adventures together. She was broken, just as I was broken, but with the help of wonderful people—and in Maybelle's case an incredibly handsome hero by the name of Arthur Lewis—we were both able to find our new 'normal'.

I do hope you find Maybelle and Arthur's story of being brave, of taking a step into the unknown, a story that inspires you to also be brave when those darn curveballs make you a little unsteady on your feet.

With warmest regards,

Lucy

REUNITED
WITH HIS
RUNAWAY DOC

BY
LUCY CLARK

Published in Great Britain 2017
By Mills & Boon, an imprint of HarperCollins*Publishers*
1 London Bridge Street, London, SE1 9GF

© 2017 Anne Clark

ISBN: 978-0-263-92652-1

Our policy is to use papers that are natural, renewable and recyclable products and made from wood grown in sustainable forests. The logging and manufacturing processes conform to the legal environmental regulations of the country of origin.

Printed and bound in Spain
by CPI, Barcelona

Lucy Clark loves movies. She loves binge-watching box sets of TV shows. She loves reading and she loves to bake. Writing is such an integral part of Lucy's inner being that she often dreams in Technicolor®, waking up in the morning and frantically trying to write down as much as she can remember. You can find Lucy on Facebook and Twitter. Stop by and say g'day!

Books by Lucy Clark

Mills & Boon Medical Romance

Outback Surgeons

English Rose in the Outback
A Family for Chloe

The Secret Between Them
Her Mistletoe Wish
His Diamond Like No Other
Dr Perfect on Her Doorstep
A Child to Bind Them
Still Married to Her Ex!

Visit the Author Profile page
at millsandboon.co.uk for more titles.

For the people who are *always* there to hold my hand when I doubt myself—Melanie, Austin, Cassie and Kate.

Thank you for your support this past year.

Proverbs 19:1

Praise for
Lucy Clark

'A good and enjoyable read. It's a good old-fashioned romance and is everything you expect from Medical Romance. Recommended for Medical Romance lovers and Lucy Clark's fans.'

—*Harlequin Junkie* on
Resisting the New Doc In Town

'I really enjoyed this book—well written, and a lovely romance story about giving love a second chance!'

—*Goodreads* on
Dare She Dream of Forever?

PROLOGUE

MAY FLEMING STOOD at the top of the stairs, fear starting to grip her as she listened to her parents speak in muted tones with the two men who had arrived only twenty minutes ago. Closing her eyes, she listened to try and grasp the gist of the conversation but all she could hear were words like 'leave', 'danger', 'tonight'.

What was going on? Was this anything to do with the break-in they'd had at their house a month ago? Her father had played down the incident, saying there had been a spate of robberies in the neighbourhood of late and as nothing had been taken it was of little consequence, but who broke into a house and didn't take anything? She knew he'd been trying not to worry her and when she'd questioned her friend Clara, who lived next door, Clara hadn't heard anything about robberies in the neighbourhood.

Add to that fact that since that attempted robbery, both of her parents had been acting more weirdly than usual lately. Sometimes they didn't come home for dinner, telling her to eat next door at Clara's house, and when they were home they were locked away in either her mother's or father's study, their voices sometimes rising to hysteria. 'Shh. You'll wake May,' her father had said to her mother just three nights ago. It had been too late for that warning. May had been woken fifteen minutes earlier by her mother's loud sobbing.

The door to the lounge room started to open and May fled from the top of the stairs to her bedroom, quickly closing the door behind her and leaning against it. Had they heard her? Was she going to be in trouble? Her parents weren't the usual type of parent. They didn't care if she stayed up all night, watching television, as long as her grades were good. If she wanted to shower at three o'clock in the morning, they were fine with that, as long as she wasn't late heading out to school in the morning.

Education was vitally important to them and, whilst May knew they loved her, they both loved their scientific researching careers more. She was OK with that because it did afford her a lot of freedom. Tonight she'd had a shower and washed her hair, hearing the doorbell ring just after she'd turned off the hairdryer.

Unsure whether she'd be required to head downstairs to meet whoever was dropping around at ten o'clock at night, she'd dressed in three-quarter-length jeans and a T-shirt, choosing not to be introduced to her parents' friends whilst wearing her pyjamas.

But she hadn't been asked to come downstairs and the firmly closed lounge room door, plus the panic in her mother's voice, had helped May to decide to stay well out of sight. Had she succeeded?

She listened, hearing the lounge room door close again, and when she ventured back out to peek downstairs, it was to see the hallway was dark and the deep-toned discussion had continued. Straining to hear, she heard the words 'tonight' being used again and again. 'It isn't safe', 'security must be maintained', 'act now'. Those were some of the other phrases and all of it was enough to cause the knot of apprehension and fear in May's stomach to expand.

She headed back to her room but the four walls started to close in around her as she tried to figure out what was going on downstairs. Shaking her head, she headed to her balcony, needing to be anywhere but here. Her parents had given her the room upstairs with the balcony, the room that would usually be considered the main room of the house, whilst their bedroom was sandwiched between their two studies so they could work long hours into the night and not disturb her. As a young girl, she'd felt like a princess in a tower, waiting for her prince to come and rescue her. As she'd entered her teens, she'd decided not to wait for anyone to rescue her but to learn how to rescue herself.

She and Clara had figured out how to shimmy up and down the poles of the balcony and now, after May had pulled on her sandshoes, she slung a leg over the railing and retraced the path she'd used so many times before.

Over the rail, down the pole, keeping to the shadows of the back garden so she didn't trigger the light sensors of the security lights her parents had installed after the break-in. She climbed the shoulder-high wire fence that marked the border between the houses and quickly ran across to the large gum tree in the Lewises' yard, the cool breeze soothing her skin, helping her to gain some sort of clarity. The old gum had nice long branches, thick enough for her to carefully make her way across, then with one large step she made it to the ledge that was next to the open window of Arthur's room.

'May!' He placed his hand over his heart and she wasn't sure whether it was because she'd startled him or the fact that his heart belonged to her. She desperately wanted to think it was the latter. Here he was. Her Arthur. Her knight. He made her feel so needed, so desirable and so precious. She'd never known a feeling like that before, and even though she'd had a crush on him for the past few years, she'd never, in her wildest dreams, thought he'd ever like her back.

But on her sixteenth birthday, just a few short months ago, Arthur had let her kiss him. Not only that but he'd kissed her back, as though something inside him had snapped and he'd finally given in to the sensations of desire. Since then, they'd been sneaking around, not wanting to tell people—even Clara—about their relationship just yet. May hadn't wanted the fact that she was dating Clara's older brother to ruin her friendship with Clara.

Now, as she looked at him, *her Arthur*, time seeming to stand still for that split second, she drank in everything about him. How could this relationship go wrong? They were perfect for each other.

He was dressed in an old pair of shorts with rips and holes in them, ones his mother had forbidden him to wear outside the house. The T-shirt he wore was equally as comfortable and, given it had been a stinking hot summer in Victoria that year, it wasn't surprising he was dressed like that. His legs were long, his feet were bare, the desk in his room was littered with papers and the bed sheets were rumpled with more study notes on them. She knew he had an exam tomorrow and that he'd told her he needed to study, but right now she didn't care about anything except being with him.

When she was in Arthur's arms, everything in her world made sense. With the way her parents had been jittery and argumentative lately, it was little wonder she wanted to feel protected. Usually, her scientist parents spent a good portion of their time at their research labs, meaning that May, instead of staying in the large two-storey house all on her own, spent most of her time next door with the Lewis family.

Being with them, with Clara and Arthur and their parents, always welcomed and included in everything they did, from outings during the holidays to eating dinner in the evening, made May feel like she was living in a normal family, rather than with scatterbrained parents who often forgot to go to the grocery store.

Spending time with the Lewis family, and in particular with Arthur, made her feel wanted and loved, and as he stood there, staring at her, she wanted nothing more than to feel his comforting arms around her, to feel the touch of his hair with her fingertips and to have his lips pressed firmly to her own in a reassuring kiss.

Having overheard words such as 'danger', 'leave', 'tonight', from the conversation in her parents' lounge room, was it any wonder May wanted to feel secure? She covered the distance between them and wrapped her hands around his neck, urging his head down so their lips could meet.

The instant she felt the pressure of his lips on hers, May began to relax. This was where she belonged. In his arms, with his mouth on hers. Her teenage heart sang for joy when he immediately kissed her back, his arms coming around her, holding her close as though he, too, was desperate to be with her. Her heart soared with love and she deepened the kiss, wanting to know everything, wanting to experience everything, wanting to feel everything.

Something big was going on next door at her house, her parents behaving crazily, but here with Arthur she was lost in the bubble of belonging and she never wanted it to end. On and on she kissed him, edging him backwards, closer to his bed so they could lie down together, could *be* together because surely doing something like that for the very first time would help her to forget everything else.

'What…?' He eased away from her, staring into her face as though he couldn't quite believe she was here and kissing him in such a way. Never, in the few months they'd been sneaking kisses and sharing touches, had she ever been this forward. As she was a few years younger than him, she'd always let him guide her, but tonight she needed to take charge, to let him see just how much she loved him, how much she wanted him. That's what all guys wanted, right?

'What's going on? What are you doing here?'

'I want you, Arthur.' She went to kiss him again but he stopped her. She closed her eyes, not wanting him to stop her. She didn't want to think things through, she didn't want to be rational and reasonable. She simply wanted to feel, to lose herself in him, in the sensations that being with him evoked throughout her entire being.

'Whoa. Wait a second.'

She let him talk and she answered him and all the while she needed to keep her thoughts focused on him, on the here and now. The words 'danger', 'leave', 'tonight' were trying to force their way to the surface and even though she didn't understand what it all meant, her intuition told her it wasn't good. She had no idea how she could explain any of this to Arthur, how she could let him know what was going on at her house, because she had no real idea herself.

She didn't want him to tell her she was overreacting, that she was allowing her imagination to get the better of her, that she should go back home and they could talk about it more in the morning. He kept glancing at his bedroom door and she knew he was skittish about having her here this late in the evening. Although his parents had no real cause to come into their son's bedroom at this hour of the night, no doubt presuming he was studying for his coming exams, there was still the possibility they might and it was clearly making Arthur more than a little nervous.

All she wanted was to lose herself in him and when the opportunity presented itself she managed to kiss him once more, letting him know through her actions, rather than her words, just how determined she was.

She loved the way his fingers tangled in her hair, the way his mouth felt on hers, the way he kissed her with such hunger and passion. He felt the same way she did. She was certain of it. Although he'd never told her exactly how he felt, the fact that he hadn't put a stop to them sneaking around and spending time together showed her just how much he really did like her.

They were so caught up with each other, her mind focusing on nothing but the way he was making her feel, that when he touched the waistband of her three-quarter-length jeans she froze for a split second, a new thrumming starting to pulse through her mind. *This was really happening!* She was going to lose her virginity here—*tonight...right now*!

Arthur paused. 'What's wrong?' He stared at her and she tried as hard as she could to let him see that she wanted this, that she wanted to be with him, to forget about everything else in the world except for the two of them and the way they made each other feel. 'We don't have to do this.'

But she wanted to. Why couldn't he realise that? It was just that it was so...so...grown-up and scary, in a good way. She tried to reassure him but even then she stammered over her words. If only she hadn't overheard what was being said in her parents' lounge room...'danger', 'leave', 'tonight'... If only she and Arthur had more time, to let their relationship develop into an even deeper sensation of passion and love, but the fear that things were going to change drastically was something she couldn't shake.

'Honey, you don't need to do anything. I'm not going to force you.'

'Oh, I know you would never do that. Never.' Her words

were clear and to the point. He brushed her hair back from her face and bent to kiss her mouth once more.

'Then why? Why come here and say what you did when you clearly have reservations?'

'Because I don't want to die a virgin!' she blurted out.

'Die? Who said anything about you dying? I'm not going to let anything bad happen to you and, besides, where you and I are concerned, we have plenty of time. Things will take their natural course when we're *both* ready.' Arthur's lips quirked a little at the corners and instead of getting cross at him for finding what she'd said amusing, she relaxed, his humour showing her she was probably overreacting.

'I know.' She extracted herself from his arms and shifted so she could lie on his bed, her head on his pillow. She absent-mindedly wound her hair around her finger, something she often did when she was confused or agitated. 'It's just that…my parents have been acting strange lately.' At Arthur's raised eyebrow, she amended, 'Stranger than usual.'

'Stranger than spending more time at their research lab than with their daughter?'

'Hey, I don't mind. It means I get to hang out here and your parents treat me like another daughter, and Clara and I can have fun together, and you and I…' she winked at him '…get to have fun together, too.'

'Don't tease,' he growled as he came to lie down next to her, slipping his arm under her head. The intense moment had passed and now, as they lay there, the atmosphere was one of friendship and support between a boyfriend and girlfriend. 'It's the way they don't seem to take much of an interest in you, as though you're always the afterthought, that I don't like. Apart from that, I think your parents are both incredibly intelligent people who will one day find a cure for cancer.'

'Perhaps they already have,' May murmured. Was that the reason her parents had been so closed off lately? Installing extra security around the house? Huddling together whilst having wildly gesticulating conversations? Had they found a cure for cancer and someone didn't want them to share it?

'Really?'

'I don't want to talk about them,' she told him. 'Tell me about your exam. Are you supposed to be studying now?'

'Yes. I was timing myself with the answers.' He pulled his watch from his pocket and May immediately put it onto her wrist.

'What subject?'

'Biology.'

'Ah. That's my speciality. I'll help you study. Where are your papers?'

'I think you're lying on them.'

'Oh.' She shifted around and pulled them out from beneath her, making sure they didn't rip. 'All right. Question number one,' she said in her best gameshow-host voice and the two of them laughed.

'Shh. We don't want my parents coming in.' He kissed her nose and she snuggled closer to him, breathing him in.

'You smell good.'

'I don't think that information is included in my revision notes.'

'I'll soon fix that.' May pulled a small pink pen from the pocket of her three-quarter-length pants, having left it in there from school that day, and wrote, 'Arthur smells delicious' in pink ink at the top of the page. 'All fixed,' she said, and handed him the pen so she could hold the papers more easily. 'OK, future Dr Lewis. Time to study.'

'I'd rather spend more time kissing you,' he returned.

'And that will be your reward because I'm not having you fail this exam because of me.' She scanned his notes. 'OK. Answer this.' She chose a question and waited for him to answer. Whenever he got it right, she kissed him. Several times she asked him questions that weren't contained within his notes, making him think even harder on the subject.

'How do you know all this stuff?' Arthur chuckled as he kissed her once more.

'Are you kidding me? With one parent researching the human genome and the other an expert in synthetic compounds, is it little wonder this stuff runs through my veins?'

'You should study medicine.'

'And become a doctor like you're going to be?'

'I'll be a couple of years ahead of you at medical school so we could study together.'

'Like you help me study for my school exams?' May giggled, remembering how their last study session had ended with the two of them making out on the couch. 'I'd never pass!'

'Sure you would. You're smart.'

May eased back and looked him. 'You think I'm smart?'

He seemed surprised by her question. 'May, you're the smartest girl I know. Why else would I be with you?'

'Because I'm pretty?'

'Honey, you're beautiful. My belle.' He kissed her. 'And yes, there's no denying we're attracted to each other, but one of the main things I love about you is your intelligence.'

'Love?' Her eyes widened at the word. 'You love me?' May's voice broke on the last word but she didn't care. Inside, her heart was soaring as high as the highest bird on a cloudless day.

'Yes.' His grey eyes were intense, his words quiet and sincere. 'Problem?'

'No. No.' She shook her head, a wide, silly grin pulling on her lips before he kissed her. She kissed him back, deciding that this was most definitely the best night of her life. Arthur loved her. Arthur *loved* her and she loved him back. It was as though her life was finally starting to make sense—as if she'd found the one place where she belonged.

'You know I love everything about you,' she said a moment later, the two of them a little breathless. 'Except for the fact that your knee is digging into my leg.' She tried to shift a little, to get comfortable so she could take his weight on top of her, but as she did so he shifted as well, almost tumbling off the bed. In order to stop himself, he reached out a hand to his bedside table for support but in the process accidentally knocked his clock off.

The clattering noise as it fell onto the polished floorboards made them both freeze. Holding their breaths, they stared at each other, waited to see if his parents had heard the noise. With the sound of a door being opened and footsteps heading towards Arthur's room, they both scrambled like wildfire, moving fast. May headed towards the window, whilst Arthur righted the clock and picked up the scattered biology papers they'd previously knocked to the floor.

May just made it out the window and over to the branch of the tree, completely out of sight, when his father opened the bedroom door.

'You all right?' his dad asked.

'Yeah, yeah. Just dozed off while trying to cram this information into my brain,' Arthur remarked, shaking the biology papers with his hand. 'The sooner this exam is over, the better.'

His father laughed then said goodnight to his son, closing the door behind him. May waited, almost willing Arthur to come over to the window. He did just that and she edged off the branch to meet him there. He kissed her through the open frame. 'You'd better go.'

'I know.' She kissed him again, putting all her love and heart into the action. 'I love you, Arthur Lewis.'

'And I love you, May Fleming. Now go. Get to bed and I'll see you tomorrow.'

With a giddiness of epic proportions, May shimmed down the tree, climbed the fence and was soon scaling her balcony as though her feet had wings. The instant she stepped inside her bedroom she froze, her giddiness turning to ice as she saw both her parents were standing in her room. The light was on, her mother's face was ashen and her father's jaw was clenched more tightly than she'd ever seen before. She was in trouble now!

'May. Oh, my goodness. There you are.' Her mother dragged her close and hugged her so tightly May thought she might pass out.

'We thought they'd got you already.' Her father wrapped his arms around his two girls. 'Don't ever scare us like that again.'

May wasn't sure what was going on except she was positive this wasn't the way normal parents disciplined their child for sneaking out of the house. A moment later she realised her mother was crying and her father was shaking.

'What's…?' She stopped, not sure she wanted to ask what was going on because she wasn't sure she wanted to hear the answer. Instead she said, 'Why are you crying?'

'Oh, May.' Her mother kissed her head. 'I'm so sorry.'

'We need to get things organised,' a deep voice said

from the doorway, and that was when May realised they weren't alone. The dread that had caused her to run to Arthur in the first place returned with full force as she eased back from her parents and stared at the dark-suited figure.

'Pack only what's necessary for now. The agency will pack the rest once you're safe.'

'Safe?' May swallowed, trying to control her rising panic.

'You're all in *danger* You need to *leave* here. *Tonight.*'

CHAPTER ONE

MAYBELLE FREEBOURNE ALL but strutted into Victory Hospital in one of Melbourne's outer suburbs. She had finally returned to the last place she could remember being truly happy. She grinned to herself at the thought. It wasn't necessarily the *hospital* that made her feel happy but rather the memories of the suburb where the hospital was located.

She stood in the middle of the new and improved hospital lobby and looked around. Victory Hospital was a medium-sized teaching hospital with all the required medical and surgical departments, but it was nowhere as big as the Royal Melbourne Hospital situated in the heart of Melbourne City about an hour away. It would do her just fine.

Maybelle wanted to get lost in the crowd but not swallowed by it. She already knew how to blend in, how to adapt her looks and personality to be accepted by her colleagues. When you'd lived a life where you were forced to relocate every two to three years, you became good at it. There was a determination about her, a determination she hadn't felt in a long time, and it felt good. Her life was finally her own. That was a good thing…right?

She wasn't going to focus on just how she'd achieved such freedom. If she did that, she risked her thoughts spiralling down a black hole it was almost impossible to get out of. *Almost* impossible. The psychologist had said she was doing exceptionally well, given everything she'd been through.

Focusing her attention on the hospital walls, noting the renovations that had vastly upgraded and improved the overall aesthetics of the building, her mind compared it to how it had looked when she'd been eight years old. She'd been rushed into the emergency department in the wee hours of the morning with appendicitis, her scientist parents beside themselves with worry. They'd been smart people when it came to the human genome and synthetic molecules but actually seeing their daughter sick had made them both feel ill.

Nevertheless, that stay in hospital had highlighted many things for young Maybelle, the main one being that she loved the way the hospital seemed to function like its own little world, from the cleaners all the way up to the surgeons and everyone in between. While both her parents had encouraged Maybelle from her very first Christmas to be a scientist, especially as they'd given her a plastic Petri dish as a gift, her mother had been astounded when Maybelle had declared she'd wanted to be a doctor.

'But there's a lot of blood with medicine and during your medical training you'll be working on cadavers.' Her mother had paused for effect. 'A cadaver is a dead person, sweetie. You don't want to be around dead people.'

'She can make up her own mind, Samantha,' her father had chimed in, looking up from the scientific journal he'd been reading. 'Just because you and I don't like dealing with people and would rather spend time with a microscope, there's no reason why she can't be a doctor. Besides…' he'd fixed her with an indulgent look '…you're only eight, sweetie. You might change your mind when you're older.' Then he'd given her mother a look that said it was best to drop the subject and her mother had done just that.

Of course, when Maybelle had finally graduated from medical school, her parents had been incredibly proud of her.

'I don't know how you do it, sweetie,' her mother had stated one night when Maybelle had returned from a long night in Emergency. 'But I like it that you're helping people, saving lives.' She met her daughter's gaze. 'Especially after everything we've put you through.'

Maybelle had hugged her mother close. Ever since they'd been put into witness protection, it had forced the three of them to spend a lot more time together, and in some ways the close family Maybelle had always wanted was what she'd finally received.

'Silver linings,' her father had often declared. 'We need to look for the silver linings in our day-to-day lives, especially if we've had a bad day.'

As it turned out, her parents hadn't discovered a cure for cancer. Instead, they'd discovered something that could cause death and devastation on a mass scale if it fell into the wrong hands. The break-in at their house had been because the thieves had been looking for her parents' research. Maybelle had found out many years later that there had also been several break-ins at their laboratory. The government had offered to protect her family, if her parents continued to work for them, creating antidotes and staying out of sight.

'Our work may never be published under our own names but we're alive,' her father would continue when he was on one of his silver-lining speeches.

'And May was able to get through medical school with only two relocations,' her mother would add. 'One day she'll be free of all this and able to start her own life—her *real* life.'

'That day has come, Mum,' Maybelle whispered to Victory Hospital's walls before she headed towards the bustling emergency department, which was located on the other side of the lobby. Sure, things had changed but she'd changed a lot, too. It was the perfect mix.

She swiped her new pass card through the security lock and pushed the door open. On the other side, her excitement waned as she glanced around the very non-bustling ED. She was pumped, ready for action, and yet there were several medical staff at the desk, which was located in the middle of the treatment bays, chatting and laughing together. No action. No franticness. No calls of 'Grab the crash cart', or 'Get the doctor here, *stat*'. Several of the treatment bays were indeed full but with patients who were now stable and being monitored.

With a deflated sigh, she headed towards the desk. She hated quiet and controlled environments. She liked busyness and movement and being rushed off her feet. None of the staff looked her way as she approached. Instead it appeared they were all listening intently to someone who was telling what must be an enthralling story.

'And then,' she heard a deep male voice say, 'she stepped on the ball!'

At the delivery of the line, everyone laughed and the spell was broken. It was then that one of the staff turned and saw her standing there. The woman jumped and placed a hand over her heart.

'Good heavens, you scared me. You must walk very quietly.'

Maybelle paused for a second, remembering how she'd been taught to sneak around places, to be inconspicuous, to make herself unnoticeable, but this time she hadn't been doing it on purpose. She held up her identification badge. 'New doctor. Officially start work in…' Maybelle glanced at the clock on the wall '…about thirty seconds' time.'

'Oh, you must be Dr Freebourne. Uh… May, is it?'

'Maybelle,' she instantly corrected, and held out her hand.

'I'm Gemma, the ED ward clerk, and I have your paperwork…somewhere here.' Gemma quickly shook Maybelle's hand, then started shuffling papers around on the desk. 'Ah. Here it is.'

'Did you say you were starting work?' one of the nearby nurses questioned. 'Fantastic. We've been so short-staffed of late.'

'Hospitals are always short-staffed,' another nurse mumbled in a matter-of-fact tone.

Gemma gathered the different pieces of paper together and held them out to the man who, Maybelle belatedly realised, had been the one enthralling the staff with his stories. 'Here you go, Arthur.'

Upon hearing the name—Arthur—something clicked in Maybelle's long-term memory. *Arthur?* It wasn't a very common name nowadays—in fact, it was still considered rather old-fashioned—but the only Arthur she'd ever known had been named after a beloved family grandfather and, as such, he'd worn the name with pride.

Her Arthur. Her King Arthur. The first boy she'd ever loved. She smiled at the memory the name brought to mind but schooled her thoughts as her new colleagues started asking her questions.

'What did you say your name was?' one of the nurses asked.

'This here,' Gemma interrupted before Maybelle could get a word out, 'is Dr Maybelle Freebourne. She joins us from a very busy and hectic teaching hospital in the heart of Sydney.' Several of the staff, who were a mix of doctors, nurses and interns, listened to Gemma's introduction before shaking hands with Maybelle and introducing themselves. This was just the sort of thing Maybelle wasn't used to—this intimate attention. It made her feel as though she were under a microscope, that they'd want to know everything about her, and she most certainly didn't want to tell anyone *everything* about her. However, it couldn't be helped. She'd made her choice and was determined to make her life work.

'Maybelle?' The deep voice that had spoken her name made her look at the man who had spoken it. He was tall, about six feet four inches. He wore navy-blue scrubs with a white coat over the top, and a stethoscope around his neck. His hair, which had once been blond, was now a light brown, peppered at the sides with a hint of distinguished grey. His nose was slightly bent, indicating a break in the past, but it was his grey eyes that caused her mouth to go dry and her heart to momentarily skip a beat. There was no way she would ever forget those eyes. How could she when they'd once looked at her with such tenderness?

'That's a very old-fashioned name,' Arthur stated.

'Like you can talk,' Gemma interjected, as Maybelle continued to stare at the man before her. 'Arthur's an old-fashioned name, too. You two will fit perfectly together. Maybelle and Arthur.'

'Old-fashioned names are making a comeback,' one of the nurses said, and began talking about how her friend was pregnant and quite a few of the baby books had many of those old-fashioned names in them and… Maybelle wasn't listening to a word.

Instead, all she could hear was the thrumming of blood pumping wildly throughout her system, reverberating in her ears, causing her heart rate to increase. It *was* the same

Arthur. This was the same boy who had lived next door to her so many years ago but now…he was even more devastatingly handsome. She couldn't help but drink her fill of the man before her.

Why, oh why, hadn't she questioned her government case worker more closely? When the paperwork had been prepared for the transfer to Victory Hospital, to her new life, Maybelle had only enquired about the CEO, not the director of the ED! However, it was too late to back out now and as his warm hand enveloped hers in the normal way of greeting, sparks spread up her arm, flooding throughout her body. If she'd had any doubt whether this Arthur was the same man who had been her first crush so many years ago, it fled with that one simple touch.

'I'm Arthur. Arthur Lewis. Director of the ED.'

Arthur Lewis and his sister Clara. What fantastic times they'd had together. She and Clara had been soul sisters and for a long while Arthur had been the big brother she'd never had…that was until she'd started to see him as something *more* than a surrogate big brother.

Maybelle cleared her throat and forced her mind back to the present, extracting her hand from his as though the touch had slightly burnt her. She quickly pushed her fingers through her short blonde curls and tried hard not to fidget. Fidgeting had always been a sure-fire sign she was uncomfortable in a situation, unsure how to proceed. *Not* a good first impression to make when starting a new job.

'Pleased to meet you, Arthur.' She took a small step back, needing to put some distance between them. She dragged in a deep breath in an effort to try to calm her senses, belatedly realising it was the wrong thing to do. Her senses were treated to the spicy, hypnotic scent she'd always equated with him. Any time she'd smelt that particular type of aftershave, she'd always thought of Arthur. Darn her smell receptors!

'Ready to start work?' He turned and gathered a few sets of case notes from the desk. 'Come into my office and we can have a chat.' He smiled at her then, an impersonal, polite smile that indicated he had no idea of her true identity. Good. This was a new beginning for her but what she hadn't expected was to be immediately confronted with her past.

Maybelle followed Arthur to his office, the name plate on his door confirming his full name—Arthur Lewis— and that he was indeed the director of the ED. Now that she'd overcome her initial shock, a part of her was secretly delighted to see what twenty years had done to him.

He offered her a seat then sat behind the well-organised desk and put on a pair of wire-rimmed glasses. Maybelle couldn't help the smile that touched her lips at seeing him wearing glasses. It made him look like his father.

'Something funny?' he asked, and it was then she realised he was watching her.

'No. No. I like your glasses,' she proffered.

'Uh…thank you.' His brow puckered a little as though he wasn't quite sure how to respond. 'Anyway, let me have a quick look over the paperwork, make sure everything is signed in the right places and that your security clearance is up to date.'

'I used my identity badge to gain access to the ED so I'd say that's a "yes".'

'Good.' He finished looking over her papers, added his own signature to two pieces of paper and then took off his glasses. 'We've had an issue with some of the staff having problems with their passes. The CEO is looking into the situation but between you and me the system does need an upgrade. However, if you have an issue where you can't gain access or get stuck somewhere, just let me know.'

'OK. Thanks for the heads-up.'

Arthur folded his hands together and looked at her intently. Maybelle tried to remain calm, tried not to do anything that might give away her true identity. Could he see it? Could he find some resemblance to the sixteen-year-old girl he'd once known?

She waited for Arthur to speak but instead he simply sat there, staring at her as though he really was seeing a ghost—and well he might be.

'Have we met?' The words seem to tumble out of his mouth before he could stop them.

Maybelle slowly shook her head. 'I—uh—'

'You just seem oddly familiar.'

She shrugged and forced a polite smile. 'I guess I have one of those faces.'

He stared at her for another long moment, as though desperately trying to place her, before leaning back in his chair. 'Anyway, do you have any questions about the ED? I'm presuming you've familiarised yourself with the hospital and departmental protocols?'

'Absolutely, and everything seems straightforward.'

'Good. Well, until you learn your way around, don't be afraid to ask for help.'

'Will do.' She wasn't sure whether to stand, whether to keep sitting until she was dismissed or whether he wanted to talk to her some more. Maybelle played with one of the curls by her ear, winding it around her ear, then realised what she was doing and forced her hands into her lap, clenching them tightly together.

The phone on Arthur's desk rang and he quickly answered it. 'Yes, Gemma.' He paused then nodded once.

'We'll be right there.' He put the phone down and stood in one swift motion.

'Three ambulances on their way, re-routed here from the Royal Melbourne. They're inundated and we're empty.' Maybelle stood and watched him walk to his office door and open it. 'Well, Dr Freebourne, there's nothing like throwing you in at the deep end. Let's see how well you swim.'

'You'll be watching me closely, I take it?' she asked as she preceded him through the door. Why had her voice sounded so intimate and soft as she'd spoken the words? 'I mean with regard to how I handle the situation,' she amended.

His answer was a small, deep chuckle that made goose-bumps tingle up and down her spine. The same laugh… but richer. This new Arthur was already proving to be a distraction and right now she didn't need any of those, especially if he was going to be monitoring the way she performed her job.

'I knew what you meant, Maybelle, but you can take it any way you like,' he remarked as they strode to the nurses' station, then he looked at her over his shoulder and winked before turning his attention to Gemma. 'What's going on?' he asked the ward clerk. As Gemma spoke, Maybelle's mind tried to decipher why he'd done that.

Why had he winked at her? What did it mean? Had he simply been teasing? He'd always been one to joke around but never to the point where it caused anyone pain. Given the way he'd been joking with his staff when she'd arrived, and the way everyone in the department seemed to be re-laxed with each other, it seemed that Arthur Lewis was still the type of man to put people at ease with a touch of humour. Was that what the wink had meant? Did it mean that he'd be watching her from a professional point of view, evaluating her skills as an emergency specialist, or did it mean he was more than willing to watch her from a non-professional point of view?

Even the thought made her body warm with anticipation as her mind dredged up the memory of exactly what it had been like to be kissed by those luscious lips of his. She also couldn't deny the effect that the wink had had on her. Arthur Lewis…winking at her in that easygoing manner of his, of teasing her, laughing with her. It hadn't been the first time he'd ever winked at her and the action was having the same devastating effect on her equilibrium as it had in the past. Darn the man for being so incredibly handsome and making her feel all feminine. She needed to concentrate on her work, not on how he could still ignite her senses with one simple action.

When Arthur started briefing the staff on the present situation, Maybelle was relieved when her mind clicked over into professional mode. Concentrating on the impending arrival of the patients, of what was expected of her, of who she would be working with, was definitely a welcome diversion from reflecting on how Arthur Lewis made her *feel*.

'There's been a bad accident on the freeway where a semi-trailer jack-knifed across the road, collecting several cars in its wake. From the reports, there are still several people trapped in their cars and the emergency service teams are doing their best to get them out. The Royal Melbourne ED is backed up with patients from other accidents from the morning commute, hence why we're getting the overload.'

'Do we know what the semi-trailer was carrying?' Maybelle interjected. 'What cargo? Was it a tanker with chemicals or fuel inside, or was it transporting animals?' She spread her hands wide. Arthur looked over at Gemma, who quickly flicked through the notes she'd taken.

'It was a tanker. Petrol tanker.'

'Good question, Maybelle,' Arthur pointed out, and she could have sworn there was an impressed quirk to his eyebrow. 'This means the possibility of burn injuries as well as the general car-related injuries such as whiplash, fractures, bruises and concussion.'

Arthur continued with his briefing, breaking people up into treatment teams and giving specific instructions.

'Maybelle, as you're fully trained in emergency medicine, you take treatment room two. I'll be in treatment room one. We'll work tag team. Larissa, you take triage. Kate, you organise the non-life-threatening patients as they arrive,' he went on, indicating to two of the nurses who had been part of the enthralled group when Maybelle had arrived. 'Gemma's called through to Emergency Theatres to have them prepare and the wards are making room. Surgical staff are being called in and registrars from the various departments are about to be notified of the situation.'

The sound of ambulance sirens could be heard in the distance and Arthur nodded to his team, his gaze focusing on Maybelle last of all. 'Let's treat these patients.' The phone on the desk started ringing and Gemma quickly answered it. With the briefing done and patients needing their attention, everyone started to go about their assigned tasks.

'Maybelle,' Arthur said. 'You're with me. Ambulance bays, *stat.*' With that, he took off his white coat and grabbed a disposable protective gown from a box, handing another one to Maybelle.

She had the tapes tied in place over her practical trousers and light knit jumper as the first ambulance pulled into the bay. Arthur opened the rear doors as the orderlies helped the paramedics get the stretcher. 'Your patient,

Maybelle. Do the Victory proud,' he stated, and she could feel him watching her intently as she turned her attention to the paramedic, ready for the handover.

If there was one thing Maybelle had become good at over the years, it was compartmentalising her thoughts and emotions, and right now, whether Arthur was assessing her or not, she had a life to save.

CHAPTER TWO

EACH OF THE three ambulances had two patients in them and so where the Victory ED had previously been vacant, it was now bustling with activity. The nurses were doing their jobs, Larissa doing triage and Kate taking care of the non-life-threatening cases. Maybelle could hear Arthur in treatment room one speaking clearly and directly to the staff members who were assisting him. His voice was deep, melodic and calming. Even though she didn't know her way around the Victory's ED, she certainly knew her way around procedure.

'Patient is a Mr Houston Bird, sixty-two years old,' the paramedic stated as Mr Bird was wheeled into treatment room two. Maybelle and the nursing staff hooked Mr Bird up to their equipment, taking his blood pressure and measuring his oxygen saturation.

'He was trapped in his car, both legs crushed beneath the steering wheel. Firefighters cut him out. Right foot is worse than the left. BP was dropping in the ambulance but after a plasma infusion it stabilised. Wound to the head, signs of whiplash and a bruise from the seatbelt.'

'Analgesics?'

'Only the green whistle.'

'Methoxyflurane?'

'No, mythelallium. It's a new compound that does the same as methoxyflurane but costs the government less.'

'Thanks. Hello, Mr Bird,' Maybelle said firmly to the man lying before her. A large bruise was forming on his forehead where he'd obviously hit it. 'I'm Dr Maybelle Freebourne. Can you hear me?'

'Of course I can, you silly woman. You're standing right next to me. I hit my head. I'm not deaf.'

At Mr Bird's clear response, Maybelle couldn't help but smile. 'That's good news.' Having not only a response but a response with chastisement was a good sign, especially when dealing with a patient who could have a possible concussion. She'd be ordering scans of his head to ensure there was no internal bleeding and as she used her penlight torch to check his pupils, Maybelle was pleased to note they were equal and reacting to light.

The nurse, whose badge indicated her name was Cici, was cutting the clothes off Mr Bird whilst an intern was removing the temporary bandages the paramedics had put around Mr Bird's feet. From the look of them, the fourth and fifth metatarsals on the right foot would require amputation. The left foot wasn't as bad but might possibly require amputation of the little toe.

'Clean and debride the wounds,' she told the intern. 'And can we get an orthopaedic registrar here to assess Mr Bird, please?' she added as the paramedics left the room, the handover complete. 'Cross, type and match.' Another nurse entered the room to help Cici and Maybelle address her patient. 'Mr Bird, have you ever been to Victory Hospital before?'

'No. No. Never before. No. I'm never sick. I'm OK. I don't know what all the fuss is about.' Mr Bird tried to shake his head as he spoke but his neck was supported by a brace, which made his efforts more cumbersome.

'Try and keep your head still until we can get some X-rays of your spine to check you haven't done any damage. Are you taking any medications you didn't tell the paramedic about?'

'What?' Mr Bird looked at her as though she was crazy. 'It's nine-thirty in the morning. The only medication I've had is my fish-oil tablet and a cup of coffee with my breakfast. How long is this going to take? I have to get to work.'

Maybelle looked across at the staff opposite her, all of them sharing a concerned look.

'Mr Bird, do you remember the accident?'

'Of course I do.' Mr Bird closed his eyes as though trying to think. 'I was driving to work—I own the company so it's imperative I get there—' He broke off, his body starting to shake and twitch.

'Mr Bird?' Maybelle looked at the read-outs from the equipment. She took the oximeter clip off Mr Bird's finger just in case he started to thrash around. The last thing they wanted when a patient was twitching in such a way was for the patient to hurt themselves so it was best they weren't connected to machinery.

'Seizure?' Cici asked. No sooner had the nurse said the word than the shaking stopped. Maybelle clipped the oximeter back and noted the change in readings.

'Push fluids. We don't want him going into shock.'

'That I get there before the rest of my staff,' Mr Bird continued as though there had been nothing wrong. It appeared he was completely unaware he'd even had a seizure. Maybelle once again checked his pupils. They were still equal and reacting to light.

'Do you remember the emergency services crews being at the accident site?' she asked her patient. There was clearly something not right. Did Mr Bird have an internal injury? She checked his reflexes and palpated his stomach.

At the touch, he moaned with pain. She'd thought his seizure might have been caused by shock but with the whack to his head she couldn't rule out something more sinister.

'They were…' Mr Bird stopped and frowned as though it was increasingly difficult for him to remember. He moaned again but this time the sound was more guttural.

'It's OK. You don't need to remember right now,' she told him gently. She needed to get him some more analgesics as well as adding a few more scans and tests to the list. 'Are you allergic to anything?'

'No.' Thought seemed difficult for him. Cici was monitoring him closely, listening to his heart and checking his blood pressure. She reported the findings. Something was definitely not right.

'Mr Bird? Can you hear me?'

'Of course I can,' he growled, his answer laced with repressed pain.

'Are you sure you're not allergic to anything?' As she asked the question, Maybelle thought back to the report from the paramedic. Mr Bird had been given a plasma infusion and the green whistle. That was it as far as medications went.

'Ugh.' He clenched his teeth. 'Uh…yes. I'm allergic to garlic but you're hardly going to serve me a meal right now.' Again his frustration was coming out in his tone and she didn't blame him.

'He's sweating,' Cici told her as she grabbed a piece of paper towel and wetted it before placing it on Mr Bird's head.

'He might vomit,' Maybelle stated. 'Do his vitals again. I need to go and check something.' While Cici took Mr Bird's vital signs once more, noting the differences, the intern finished cleaning Mr Bird's feet and placing another temporary bandage on them.

Maybelle rushed out to Gemma's desk, wanting the ward clerk to look something up on the computer, but the other woman wasn't there. She needed the computer but as there had been no time to log her into the system, she wasn't quite sure what to do next.

'Something wrong?' It was Arthur who spoke from just behind her.

'I need the computer.' There was agitation in her tone. 'I need to look up the new medicine in the green whistle.'

'Mythelallium?'

'Yes. They still use methoxyflurane in Sydney so I was unfamiliar with the new green whistle drug and I don't know…' As she spoke, Arthur sat down in the chair and quickly logged into the computer, typing the name of the drug into the system. 'Something isn't right. My patient had a small seizure and then moaned when I palpated his abdomen.'

'Any known allergies?'

'Garlic.'

Arthur raised his eyebrows as the compound breakdown of mythelallium came up on screen. 'The breakdown for mythelallium is…'

Maybelle leaned towards the computer, her shoulder touching his, but it was the words on the screen that interested her more. Arthur was rattling off a list of drugs and the second to last one was *allium sativum*.'

'Otherwise known as garlic?' she queried, and a moment later, after he'd opened another screen to check the information, they had their answer. There was a garlic synthesised compound in mythelallium.

'He's vomiting,' she heard Cici call from the treatment room.

'I need to get him an antiemetic.'

'I'll get it,' Arthur said as Maybelle rushed back to her patient.

'Mr Bird,' she said as Cici helped Mr Bird to get cleaned up. 'Mr Bird, can you hear me?'

'Yes, yes.' His voice was much weaker than before and when Maybelle looked at the readings of his pulse, heart rate and oxygen sats, she noted they'd spiked.

'Mr Bird, the medication you were given in the ambulance contains a synthesised garlic compound, which means you're having an allergic reaction to the drug.' Arthur came into the room with the antiemetic and double-checked it with Maybelle before administering it. 'This medication should help counteract the reaction and help us to stabilise you.'

Thankfully, it didn't take long for the medication to work and by the time the orthopaedic registrar arrived for the review, Mr Bird was in a much better position to receive treatment for the injuries he'd sustained during the accident.

'That was quite something,' Arthur stated, clearly impressed with the newest member of the Victory Hospital ED. Maybelle didn't want any accolades.

'Just doing my job, boss.' She returned to the nurses' desk in order to write up her notes and was thankful that Gemma was back and able to help with the computer log-in.

'How did you know?' Arthur asked, leaning against the desk next to where Maybelle was sitting.

She shrugged a shoulder and continued to input the information into the computer. There was no way she was going to mention the fact that her mother had been an expert in synthetic compounds and that Maybelle had been raised listening to her parents discussing the various ways synthetic compounds could cause reactions.

Hearing Arthur's tone should make her pleased that she'd passed the test, but instead it made her a little uneasy about having his undivided attention focused solely on her. Any time anyone gave her their undivided attention, watching her closely, intrigued by her, Maybelle's automatic response was to pull away, to put up walls, to withdraw. It was what she'd been taught to do, to remain as inconspicuous as possible… But now there was no need to hide, no need to keep such a strong distance from interacting with other people. Arthur was paying her a compliment and she needed to learn to accept them.

Drawing in a deep breath, she glanced at him and offered a small smile. 'Process of elimination. Mr Bird's reaction to the trauma already inflicted on his body wasn't within normal parameters so I simply looked for the abnormal.'

'Have you come across another patient who was allergic to garlic before?'

'No.'

'So it was a lucky guess?'

She stopped typing then and raised an eyebrow at him. 'It was a *calculated deduction*, thank you very much,' she pointed out, and received one of his delicious, rich chuckles as a reward.

'As I said, lucky guess.'

Maybelle sighed, unable to believe how happy it made her feel to be there with him, to interact with him in such a normal way. She absent-mindedly twirled her hair around one finger. 'Don't you have any more patients to attend to, Dr Lewis?'

Arthur didn't immediately answer but instead watched her closely, his brows drawing together in a frown. He paused a moment before saying quietly, 'Are you sure we haven't met before? You really do seem oddly familiar.'

His voice was quiet, as though he was trying to put the pieces of the puzzle together but couldn't remember where he'd left the jigsaw.

Maybelle instantly dropped her hand and turned her attention from him. She wished he wouldn't look at her in such a way, one that said he was intrigued by her. She didn't want to be intriguing to anyone—man, woman or child—and especially not to Arthur Lewis.

If she told him the truth, if she confessed that they really did know each other, it would only bring a plethora of questions and most of them were ones she either couldn't answer or chose not to. The past twenty years of her life had been crazy, insane and by no means normal. This meant that people who had lived a very normal, very mundane life found it nigh on impossible to understand exactly what she'd been through.

It was the reason she'd been given a new identity, a new name, a new hairstyle and even new contact lenses. What would Arthur say if she took them out? Would he recognise her more easily with blue eyes rather than the brown contacts she wore? Would he know that her name had been May Fleming rather than Maybelle Freebourne?

Even the way he was looking at her brought back memories of another time when he'd looked at her with such intensity. Back then she'd had butterflies in her stomach, sweaty palms and jelly knees. This time, though, the sensations seemed magnified as she was no longer a teenager in the throes of a silly high school crush. How was it possible she still felt a smouldering attraction to a man she hadn't seen in such a long time?

Thankfully, she was saved any further thought on the matter by the sounds of ambulance sirens in the distance as the next wave of patients was brought to their door. However, as he gave her one last quizzical look before walking away, Maybelle realised she'd probably just given herself away by not immediately answering him, by not immediately denying any claims to his questions.

'As I told you, I have one of those faces,' was what she should have said. Or she could have followed with, 'It's the haircut. It reminds people of Marilyn Monroe,' which was one she'd been planning to use, but instead all she'd done was drop her hand from the tell-tale fidget of winding her hair around her finger and look at him with an expression of trepidation lest he figured out exactly who she was.

Gritting her teeth and closing her eyes for a moment, Maybelle dragged in a deep breath, pulling her professionalism around her. She could do this. She could start a new life even with part of her old life lurking around the edges. All she had to do was to keep her personal distance from Arthur Lewis and she would be fine. It was a good plan and one she was intent on keeping.

By the end of her first shift, apart from the 'Arthur' problem, Maybelle was pleased she'd made the decision to move back to the area where she'd grown up. The staff at Victory Hospital were great and she'd managed to find an apartment only five blocks from the suburb she'd lived in all those years ago. The apartment block was close to the hospital, which meant she could walk to and from work until she managed to find time to organise a car.

Walking into her building, which housed four apartments, two upstairs and two downstairs, Maybelle knew she should be exhausted but there was still a spring in her step. All in all, today had been a good day and she'd made a point, so many years ago, to always acknowledge the good days when they came along because all too often her days hadn't been that happy.

Unlocking her front door, Maybelle headed into the furnished apartment. Yes, it was sparse, yes, there were quite a few boxes waiting for her to unpack, but she could still call it 'home'. The furniture was utilitarian but served its purpose, and she'd more than likely be spending most of her time at the hospital, rather than lounging around here, watching movies on television… At least, that was how her life had been in the past. Work, sleep. Work, sleep. Don't get involved with people. Don't be too friendly with people. Don't leave a lasting, memorable impression on people. Work, sleep. That had been her life.

However, now that she was technically free from the constraints that had governed her life, she'd come to realise she had no idea *how* to be free. Her world had been ordered, direct and absolute in so many ways with little room for deviation. The last thing her government case worker had said to her was, 'Go. Live a normal life.' The problem was, she had no idea how to do that.

Heading to the kitchen, she opened the fridge, looked at the shelves, empty except for half a container of milk, then closed it again. It was then she remembered the one thing she'd been planning to do after finishing work—go to the grocery store.

Although there were several twenty-four-hour grocery stores in the area, all of them would require her to take a taxi there and then another one back, laden with shopping bags, and she simply didn't have the energy for that. Where the ED had been quiet when she'd arrived at work that morning, it had remained at a steadily hectic pace until Arthur had ordered her to go home and let the next shift take over.

'Looks as though it's take-out time,' she told her empty apartment, but even then she wasn't sure who to call or who delivered. She could use the internet on her phone to check restaurants in the area but not only did that not guarantee a decent meal, it was also the antisocial thing to do. The only other thing she could do was to see if one of her neighbours was home, to see if they could provide some intelligence to good nearby food places or take-out menus. 'That's what a "normal" person would do,' she told herself as she headed back out of her apartment. 'They'd interact with neighbours and be friendly.' However, the apartment on the upstairs landing next to hers yielded no response to her knock.

Down the stairs she went and again received no answer from the first door she knocked on. One more door to try and if she was the only person in this building it looked as though she might be having milk for her evening meal.

Maybelle knocked on the door, whispering to herself what she was planning to say. 'Sorry to bother you. I'm your new neighbour, Maybelle Freebourne. I live upstairs and—' The door opened before she could complete her preparation and the polite smile she'd pasted onto her lips died a sudden death as she stared into the grey eyes of Arthur Lewis.

'What are you doing here?' she demanded as they stood staring at each other.

'Me?' He laughed at her question. 'I think you're forgetting that you're the one who knocked on my door, Maybelle.'

'Your door? *Your door*?'

'Yes.' Arthur pointed to the door he'd just opened.

'You *live* here?'

'I do.' It was his turn to frown. 'How did you find me?'

'I didn't. I didn't find you.' She closed her eyes and rubbed one hand over her forehead before pinching the bridge of her nose as though trying to stave off a headache. 'I can't believe *you*, of all people, live here.'

'What does that mean?' He laughed, the delightful

sound filled with utter confusion. 'Why did you knock on my door?'

She dropped her hand and opened her eyes. 'Food.' She spread her arms wide as though her answer made perfect sense.

'You want food?' He laughed again and she wished he wouldn't because the more gorgeous he sounded and the more breath-taking he looked, the harder it was for her to shut him out of her mind. 'Maybelle, I don't understand what's going on. Are you all right?'

'I'm hungry.'

'And you're just knocking on random doors, hoping someone will give you food?'

'No.' She pointed up the stairs. 'I only moved in yesterday and with the emergencies today, I didn't get around to going to the grocery store.'

'Oh, *you're* the new tenant in the building.' He stepped back from the doorway, no longer confused but still looking incredibly handsome with that sexy smile touching his lips. 'I was notified there was someone moving in but I didn't realise it was you. Well, as you're looking for food and as I'm just dishing up my dinner, please, come on in…*neighbour*.'

CHAPTER THREE

'UH...' MAYBELLE FALTERED as she stood on the threshold. Not only was she trying to wrap her head around the fact that the one man she'd wanted to keep at a distance lived downstairs but now he was inviting her to dinner! 'I...uh...don't want to intrude. I just wanted to know the phone number of a place that delivers food.'

'I understood the request, Maybelle.'

There it was again—that infuriating quirk of his lips and that twinkling brightness in his eyes that displayed his amusement at the present situation. 'Good. Well, if you wouldn't mind giving me some phone numbers or menus, I'll get out of your hair.'

Arthur stepped forward and leaned in close to her. 'What if I don't want you to get out of my hair? Ever think of that?'

At that moment, Maybelle couldn't think of *anything* due to his closeness. There it was. That glorious scent of his that made him smell like he'd come fresh from a shower, that he was a strong and confident man, that he could cope with any situation life threw at him. How she managed to get such a strong image from just the scent, she had no idea! Chances were it also had a lot to do with his own personal pheromones, his charm and his incredibly toned body, which, presently, wasn't far from her own. If she were to lean in just a touch and angle her head a little to the left then…

'Uh…' Great. She was back to faltering again. What on earth was wrong with her? Usually, she had a thousand quips, all designed to keep people at arm's length but Arthur Lewis wasn't 'people'. He was *Arthur*, and he was only trying to be neighbourly. If she made a big deal out of the situation, then it might bring more questions. Besides, doing something was better than standing here, staring at him, remembering with perfect clarity what it had been like to feel those lips against her own.

Maybelle cleared her throat. 'OK.'

'OK…what?' It was only when he spoke that she realised he'd been looking at her just as much as she'd been looking at him. A thread of panic wove through her. Had he recognised her? For one split second she couldn't remember whether she was still wearing her brown contact lenses or not. Had she taken them out when she'd arrived home? She blinked her eyes a few times then glanced down at the floor. The contacts were also prescription and as she could see things quite clearly, that tended to indicate they were still in place.

Whew! Forcing herself to think logically rather than with emotional irrationality helped calm the rising panic that Arthur had recognised her. The new persona was still firmly in place and she should stop dithering and make the decision to either stay or go. What would a new neighbour do when invited to dinner?

'OK, I'll come inside.' She glanced up at him and forced a smile.

'Oh. Good.' With that, he seemed to recover his equilibrium and stepped back to welcome her into his apartment. 'As I said, I was just about to dish up.'

Maybelle breathed in and immediately felt her stomach gurgle. Arthur heard it too and chuckled. 'I'm going to take that as a compliment, Maybelle.' He headed into the kitchen where the delicious spicy scent increased.

'What is that?' She pointed to the slow cooker sitting on the bench top. 'It smells delicious.'

'Hungarian goulash,' he told her.

'You made it?'

'Of course.' He glanced at her over his shoulder as he pulled another plate out of the cupboard. 'Cutlery's in the drawer.' He indicated the drawer in question. 'Why don't you set the table while I dish up?'

'Yes, boss,' she replied, all awkwardness fleeing in the light of having something warm and delicious to eat on such a wintry night. It was strange to be in someone else's kitchen, going through the drawers and following his instructions regarding where to find other things such as place mats and wine glasses.

'I'm hardly your boss here, Maybelle.'

'Sorry. I meant, yes, chef.'

She was rewarded with another one of his delicious chuckles. 'Better.' It didn't take him long to dish up and by the time he'd done that, Maybelle had managed to find everything she needed to set two places at the table.

'Bon appetit,' Arthur remarked as he placed a plate in front of her. Not only was there Hungarian goulash on the plate but mashed potatoes and vegetables, and everything smelled delicious.

'Thank you, Arthur. This is…this is very kind of you,' she replied, anxious to let him know that this hadn't been her plan. She was trying desperately not to think about the last time they'd been alone together…that night in his room. In some ways it felt completely right to be here alone with him, and in other ways she half expected his parents to walk in, much as his father had interrupted them so very long ago.

'Ah…my mother would be proud.' He raised his glass of wine and held it out to her.

'Your mother?'

'Yes. She done raised me good and proper like.' He clinked his wine glass to hers then chuckled at his incorrect English. Then, as though he had no idea of her turbulent emotions, he sipped his wine and started to eat his dinner.

Seeing Arthur again was one surprise she'd managed to deal with, but to hear him talk of his mother made her want to ask questions about his family. How were his parents? Were they still alive? Doing well? How was Clara? Oh, her dear, sweet friend Clara. How she'd missed Clara those first few years.

As they ate, Arthur asked very general questions about her last job in Sydney, asking her if she knew certain people. She did her best to keep her answers vague because at that last hospital she'd had a different identity. There, she'd been Margaret Adamson, working in the paediatric emergency department.

That was one thing with being in the witness protection programme organised by the government—you were able to have all sorts of papers and passports provided in the new identity they created for you. Every time she and her parents had been forced to move, another set of papers had been created and the old ones destroyed.

This last time around, with the threat to her life deemed to be over, she'd asked if she could go back to her real name, to finally become May Fleming again. Her case worker had denied the request, telling her that when they'd first been put into witness protection their true identities had been listed as void.

'There's no going back. Only moving forward. Why not choose a name that is similar to your own?'

And hence Dr Maybelle Freebourne had been created, and whilst May Fleming's experience in medicine was indeed at an exceptional level, the qualifications for Dr Maybelle Freebourne had been adjusted and printed up on new parchment paper by her case worker. There was no way she could tell Arthur any of that, so tried to change the subject, turning her attention back to the delicious food.

'There's a specific spice in your goulash that I'm having trouble pinpointing.' She took another mouthful and closed her eyes, trying to figure out what it might be. 'Hmm…cardamom?' Maybelle licked her lips and opened her eyes to find him staring at her with such intensity that her stomach flipped with nervous knots.

'Garam masala,' he stated bluntly, clearly having other topics he wanted to discuss rather than the 'secret' ingredient in the food. 'Maybelle, I know you say we haven't met before but there's something about you that is…' He stopped and shook his head. 'You're familiar to me. So much so that it felt completely natural to invite you to share a meal with me, especially when we've only just met.'

'You…ah…don't usually…' She stopped, realising her breathing was starting to increase and that she didn't want him to question why his words had flustered her. Clearing her throat, she worked hard to get her heart rate back to normal because when Arthur looked at her the way he was now, with that intriguing gorgeousness, it was almost impossible for her to not blurt out the truth.

She had to confess that she'd felt that same tug of awareness he was talking about, but she had the advantage over him as she knew exactly why she was feeling that way. Surely if she told Arthur the truth, he would understand. Yes, her case workers had assured her she was out of danger, so what would be the harm in telling him? She didn't have to lie about her true identity in order to protect him, but after years of keeping herself to herself, it was difficult for her to open up and share such an intimate confession…even with someone like Arthur, the first boy she'd ever trusted.

Her main problem now was that he was still staring at her, and very soon it was possible she'd forget all rational thought and throw herself across the table into his arms. The thrumming of her heart reverberated around her body and she found it nigh on impossible to look away from his compelling stare.

'Arthur…I…' An unexpected yapping at her heels startled her and she quickly shifted in her chair to see a gorgeous Pomeranian dog sniffing around her feet. 'Hello!' Maybelle glanced at Arthur but rested her gaze somewhere around his throat, unable to completely meet his eyes after such an intense moment. Her heart rate started to settle as she looked down at the pooch. 'I didn't realise you had a dog.'

'I don't.'

'Uh…' Maybelle put a hand down so the dog could sniff her and when the cute little thing nudged and licked her hand, Maybelle patted the soft fur. 'Then I'm clearly imagining things.' She smiled as the dog continued to lick her hand. 'What's your name, sweetie?' she asked the dog, unable to believe the complete delight she felt at the total acceptance from the animal. There was no judgement here, no need to worry about what her name used to be or what it was now. The adorable dog just accepted her and Maybelle's heart swelled with delight.

'That's Fuzzy-Juzzy. Technically, she belongs to my sister.'

'Your sister? Your sister lives here?' Maybelle's eyes

widened in astonishment, her gaze meeting Arthur's. Clara was here? Her mouth went dry at the thought. She was sixty-five percent sure she could convince Arthur they'd never met but Clara was a different story. Clara had been Maybelle's first and only best friend. Their mothers had been pregnant at the same time, with Clara being born two days before Maybelle. They'd been as close to twins as two girls could be, even to pricking their fingers and mixing their blood, proclaiming themselves to be soul sisters.

'No. She's overseas. She told me she'd be gone for six months and would I mind her dog.' As he spoke, he stood and came around the table and picked up Fuzzy-Juzzy, who was eyeing Maybelle's unfinished dinner with relish. 'That was two and a half years ago, so I guess in some ways Juzzy is mine as well.' He patted the dog. 'And you've had your dinner, Ms Juzzy.' He carried the dog from the room, giving Maybelle a moment to close her eyes and find some level of composure.

'That was close,' she whispered. Hearing that Clara was out of the country allowed Maybelle to breathe more easily. At least she didn't have to face that hurdle straight away. She opened her eyes, knowing the best thing she could do right now was to leave Arthur's apartment and return to her own. Tomorrow she would buy groceries and find out the best take-away places in the area so there would be no need for her to bother her neighbour again. She ate two more mouthfuls of the yummy food before carrying both plates to the kitchen.

It was there she found Arthur, scooping another spoonful of the goulash into Juzzy's food bowl and putting it down in the laundry, which was where the dog had obviously been eating when Maybelle had arrived.

She chuckled at the sight. 'Clearly Juzzy's used her feminine wiles on you. Clever dog. I guess it shows you really are a big softy at heart, aren't you, Dr Lewis.' The question was rhetorical but seeing the way he obviously cared for the dog warmed her. It appeared Arthur Lewis was the same in essentials as he'd been all those years ago. Thoughtful, caring and giving. It was a comforting thought.

He straightened as though he didn't like being caught in the act. 'She was whining.' His tone was a little gruff.

Maybelle laughed. 'I think it was more like she looked at you with those big brown puppy eyes of hers and you capitulated.'

He looked at the dog for a split second then shrugged his shoulders, conceding defeat on the matter. 'Or that.' Arthur put the kettle on. 'Coffee? Tea? Another glass of wine?' He wished she hadn't laughed like that. The tinkling sound had filled his apartment with vibrant colour, something he hadn't realised had been missing until that very moment. What was it about this woman that seemed so natural, so normal, so incredibly familiar?

Why did he find Maybelle Freebourne so compelling? Was it her blonde curls? Her rich brown eyes? The gorgeous smile that was still hovering on her perfectly shaped lips? Lips that, for some odd reason, he suddenly wanted to taste. He swallowed over the thought and dismissed it. They were colleagues and although he was intrigued, he also needed to keep things professional.

There was no doubt she was an excellent doctor, which she had proved most readily today with her patient, Mr Bird, but he'd also noted that she'd held herself aloof from other members of staff. Of course, with it being her first day on the job, she might want to find her feet when it came to social interaction with colleagues but the ED team was a close-knit one and he didn't want her disrupting that camaraderie with her reticence at joining in.

That close-knit atmosphere was something he'd taken time to nurture since his appointment to Director eleven months ago. The team was often called upon to work in excessively stressful situations, and knowing there was a level of trust in those types of situations was vitally important.

'Thanks but I'd better go. Dinner was absolutely delicious but I think I've imposed on you enough for one night.' She jerked a thumb towards his front door as she spoke.

Arthur wasn't sure why but he didn't want her to go. He'd enjoyed her company during dinner—a meal he either ate alone or with a heap of journal articles in front of him so he could catch up on his reading whilst eating.

'Actually, there's something I wanted to show you first.' Thinking about the journal articles had reminded him that he'd read one a few nights ago on food allergies and how to identify them in an emergency situation.

'Can you…uh…show me at work tomorrow?'

Didn't she want to stay? Why was it she seemed cagey and eager to leave? In fact, there had been several times when he'd noted his new neighbour to be a little jittery. Was that normal for her? Was she trying to leave his apartment because she found him boring? If that was the case, why on earth was he trying so hard to get her to stay?

'Is my company that bad?' The words burst from his mouth before he could stop them. She raised an eyebrow, clearly surprised.

'No. No. Not at all. I've enjoyed a lovely, home-cooked meal with *good* company.' Her words were almost over-polite. 'I simply didn't want to impose any further.' Maybelle stood with her back close to the wall, as though she didn't trust him.

'It's no imposition, Maybelle.' He watched her for another moment, noticing how she was starting to edge towards the hallway. If she didn't want to stay, he couldn't make her. 'I was reading an article about food allergies. I'd like your opinion on it.'

'Thinking of writing up Mr Bird's condition for a publication?' she queried as he headed into his bedroom. Arthur tried to quickly locate the article from the stack of medical journals on his bedside table.

'That's a possibility,' he returned, raising his voice so she could hear him. 'Perhaps we could co-author the paper, given that you were the one to discover Mr Bird's allergy in the first place.'

'And as you're the director of the ED, would that mean you'd take lead on the article?' she called back.

He paused for a second and analysed her words. Had that happened to her before? She'd done all the work and someone else had taken the credit? 'If *I* did more research and provided more information for the paper, then it would follow that my name would be lead on the article.' Where was that journal he wanted? He had the feeling that if he took too long, Maybelle would simply let herself out of his apartment and right now, he had to admit, it was great to be able to discuss a mutual topic of interest after dinner.

There was also the possibility he wanted her to stay and chat for a while so he could figure out just where he'd met her before. The few times he'd been caught staring at her, it had been as though his subconscious had been incredibly close to unlocking the memory. Perhaps they'd met years ago at a medical conference overseas. Or sat next to each other at a fundraising dinner...although if that had been the case, he was sure he would have remembered such a stunningly beautiful woman as Maybelle Freebourne.

'Do you read the *Journal*?' he called as he threw the stack of journals onto the messy bed in an effort to expedite his search. He didn't receive a reply to his question. 'Or do you prefer a different medical publication?' Still silence. He flicked through another copy of the *Journal* and finally found the article. There was no answer to his question and he half expected to find her gone when he returned to the lounge room. That, however, wasn't the case.

Instead, he found Maybelle standing at the mantelpiece next to the unlit fireplace. In her hand was a photograph of Arthur's sister Clara and her best friend. The photo had been taken at the joint sixteenth birthday party for the two girls.

'That's my sister, Clara.' Clearly Maybelle hadn't heard him walk back into the room and she spun around, her face so white it was as though she'd seen a ghost. Did Maybelle think he was mad at her for touching the pictures? 'That's not how she looks now, of course. She's a grown-up…or so she tells me, but she has such a crazy sense of humour that oftentimes I do tend to wonder.'

Arthur put the *Journal* onto the arm of the lounge and went to stand next to Maybelle. Was it his imagination or did she take a slight step away from him? 'This photograph,' he continued as he took another one off the mantel, 'was taken not long after Clara graduated from medical school. That's my parents and myself and Clara.' He held it out for her to look at and belatedly realised, when Maybelle lifted her gaze away from the picture of the two girls, that her eyes were brimming with tears.

'Maybelle? What's wrong?' Arthur put out a hand on her shoulder but she immediately flinched and backed away.

'Uh…' She sniffed and blindly shoved the photograph she'd been holding in his direction. He didn't grab it in time before she let it go, the frame falling to land on the soft carpet. 'I can't.' She was breathing fast and shaking her head as she continued to back away. There was a mixture of emotion in her eyes—surprise, trepidation, confusion mixed with a large dose of fear. 'I can't do this.' The words were barely audible before she turned and almost sprinted to the front door. Within another moment she was out and gone.

Arthur headed to the door after her, absolutely stunned at what had just transpired. What was going on? There was so much about Maybelle Freebourne that made no sense. He looked out the open front door, only to hear the door to the apartment above him close.

He shut his own door then looked down at the photograph he still held in his hand. His parents, his sister and himself, standing in front of their old family home. What had spooked her about that photo? Returning to the lounge room, he picked up the photograph she'd dropped and sat down on the lounge to study it further.

Where he'd previously thought his new colleague was something of an enigma, he now realised he didn't know the half of it. What on earth had upset her? She'd been staring at the photograph of his sister and her friend, and she'd been crying. Why? And why had she said she couldn't do this? What on earth was that supposed to mean? She couldn't socialise with her neighbours? She couldn't be friends with him outside the hospital? Perhaps looking at his family photographs had made her realise she was standing in her work colleague's apartment and that the lines of personal and professional shouldn't be crossed? What? What had happened? What had she been thinking? His mind whirred in a never-ending circle as he stared at the photographs before him.

There was the one of his family and then one of Clara and her childhood friend, May Fleming. Clara had dark brown curly hair, the curls bouncing on her shoulders in a haphazard mess, her brown eyes smiling happily. May, on the other hand, had long, straight strawberry-blonde hair with pale blue eyes. Like chalk and cheese. The two girls had been friends all their lives then, about two months after that photo had been taken, May and her parents had left the neighbourhood without a word to anyone. The house next door where they'd lived had been sold and they'd never heard from them again.

None of this reflection gave him any indication as to why Maybelle had been so distraught over the photograph. Perhaps she knew May Fleming? Had she recognised Clara's friend who had disappeared without a trace? That had to be it, or something like it, and from the way Maybelle had reacted when she'd seen the photograph, things hadn't ended well for young May.

That thought alone made him feel sick to his stomach. Poor May. Being only two years older than Clara, he'd grown up with May around all the time. She'd been like another little annoying sister to him...until the evening that photograph had been taken.

Arthur put his head back and closed his eyes. May. Young, gorgeous and quietly sassy. He'd known she'd had a crush on him and that night, with everyone else enjoying the outdoor sweet-sixteen party in his parents' backyard, he'd gone against his better judgement and let her kiss him. Pushing a hand through his hair, he exhaled harshly and closed the door on the memory because not only had he let her kiss him...he'd kissed her back.

Although it wasn't too late, he had an early start in the morning and decided to get a bit of reading done after he'd tucked Fuzzy-Juzzy in her bed. It wouldn't be too much longer until Clara was back to claim her pooch but after living with the dog, Arthur had to admit he liked having Juzzy around for company. To come home to an apartment where there was no one to greet him seemed foreign now yet when Clara had begged him to take the dog all those years ago, it had been difficult to adjust to having someone around.

Sitting in his bed, he settled down to re-read the article about food allergies he'd been wanting to show Maybelle. Now, having experienced first-hand how an allergy to garlic could have drastic consequences for a patient, he read the piece with new interest. Perhaps he and Maybelle *could* investigate this further and write a paper together. He smiled at the thought. It would definitely give him time to figure out just where he knew her from. She'd obviously made an impression on him but clearly the same couldn't be said for her as she kept stating she didn't know him.

Still, he couldn't shake the feeling that she was hiding something. He made a mental note to review her job application in the morning, hoping to find some clue as to why she tended to be jittery and emotional.

I can't do this. The words she'd uttered before she'd bolted from his apartment reverberated around his mind. He closed his eyes, recalling the fear in her eyes, as though she was positive he'd already stumbled onto her secret. What secret? What was she trying to hide?

The ringing of his phone startled him from his deep thoughts and after checking the caller ID, he breathed a sigh of relief and connected the call. 'Hi, sis. How's life in the northern hemisphere?'

'Fair to middling,' Clara stated. 'Have you spoken to Mum today?'

'Not today. I spoke to Dad on the weekend.'

'Off to Italy for a holiday! Oh, the life of the retired.'

'They deserve it.'

They chatted about Clara's week before his sister asked after her dog. 'How's Juzzy? I miss her so much.'

'Then come home.' Arthur missed his sister. As it had been only the two of them growing up, whilst they'd most definitely fought and had their moments where they'd hated each other, as adults they were actually good friends. 'You said six months!'

'Yeah, I know. Sorry about that, bro.'

Arthur could hear the sadness in his sister's voice. He knew why she'd left in such a hurry and he'd hoped she was now over her broken heart. He'd sworn that if he ever saw the man who had caused Clara such distress, he'd punch him in the nose—and he was not a man prone to violence. Not only that but shortly after the relationship had ended, Clara had been in a terrible accident. Once her physical injuries had healed, she'd headed overseas with the hope of escaping her past and making new, happy memories. He needed to keep their conversation light so he chatted more about the dog. 'At any rate, Juzzy certainly likes my beef goulash.'

'You're going to make her fat, Arthur.' Clara's tone lightened as she laughed.

'So how's the life of a hectic country GP this week?'

'Hectic,' Clara replied. 'Clinics, emergencies and absolutely no respect for office hours. I'm the county doctor, which means my time and my life are not my own, they clearly belong to the village and surrounding districts.'

'So come home.'

'I said I was going to and I will.' There was still hesitation there. 'I got the email you sent about that new specialist centre opening up as part of Victory Hospital. Do you really think I'm right for the position of GP in such a busy practice?'

'Most definitely. There will be state-of-the-art equipment and the practice will be intimate yet busy enough for a workaholic like you and the fact that you did your training at the Victory and know a lot of the staff is definitely a bonus.'

'Do you know, I was just saying to my friend Imogen the other day that…' As he listened to his sister talk, Arthur's thoughts once more turned to the way Maybelle had reacted to the photographs. One of him and his family, one of Clara and May. It didn't matter how many times he'd told himself *not* to think about it, he didn't seem able to stop.

'What's wrong, Arthur?'

'Huh?'

'You're ignoring me. You only ignore me when you're completely preoccupied by something else.'

'That's not the *only* time I ignore you,' he joked.

'Very funny,' she replied drolly. 'Spit it out.'

'I don't know.' He paused, knowing this was going to sound completely strange to his sister. 'I was, uh…I was thinking about May Fleming this evening.'

'May? Wow. That's a blast from the past. Why were you thinking about her?' Clara's tone indicated she was genuinely interested, so he told his sister everything about his new colleague and neighbour, and how he'd asked her in for dinner. He told her about Maybelle's reaction to the photograph on the mantel. When he'd finished, there was silence on the other end.

'Clara? What do you think?'

'It *is* odd. Why would she drop the photo like that? And be so upset?'

'Right.' He was glad his sister thought the same way as him.

'Do you think she knew May?'

'That's the only thing that makes any sense. Do you remember anyone called Maybelle Freebourne?'

'Name doesn't ring a bell but perhaps she knew May after we did.'

Arthur paused for a moment and frowned. 'Doesn't it strike you as odd the way the Flemings just upped and left like that? Never to be heard from again?'

'I heard from May,' Clara stated.

His sister's words completely stunned him. 'What? When?'

'She wrote to me. About a month after they left. She said that her father had received a promotion overseas with his work and it had started immediately.'

'She wrote to you! You never told me that.'

'Yeah. She also sent me birthday cards for a few years but then they stopped.'

'Was there ever a return address?'

'No.'

'So you had no way of contacting her?'

'No, but in the last birthday card she sent she wrote that she hoped one day we could meet again and that I would forgive her.'

'For what?'

'For leaving, I guess.'

'Why didn't I know any of this?'

'Because every time I even mentioned May's name in passing you'd bite my head off, just like you are now!'

Arthur leaned his head back on the pillows and closed his eyes, slowly exhaling. 'Sorry, sis.'

'Go to sleep, bro. It sounds like you need it. Clear your head and tackle the problem fresh tomorrow.'

'Can you at least try to remember if you know someone called Maybelle Freebourne?'

'This woman's really got you in a spin, hasn't she?' Clara chuckled. 'You like her.'

'Stop it.'

'It's about time you got back in the game, bro.'

'You can talk.' There was no way he was discussing

his love life, or lack thereof, with his sister. But she did have a point.

'Yeah, we're both hopeless cases. Anyway, I've got to go. Patients are starting to arrive for clinic. I'll talk to you soon.'

Arthur said goodbye to his sister then tried to control his thoughts by reading, but after reading the same sentence fifteen times he closed the publication and shook his head. He simply couldn't stop thinking about Maybelle's reaction to that photo. Something very odd was going on and he didn't like unsolved mysteries.

May's disappearance was an unsolved mystery. He could see it all so clearly in his mind, himself and May, standing beneath the foliage at the end of the garden, twinkle lights creating a festive environment. There had been so many people there—a joint sixteenth birthday party— that May had assured him no one would miss them.

'I just need to talk to you for a minute or two,' she'd told him, taking his hand and leading him to the end of the garden. Arthur had looked around to see who might be watching them but they'd escaped unseen.

'I'm not sure we should be—' he'd begun, but she'd pulled him further into the foliage and then pressed a finger to his lips to silence him.

'I have a very special birthday wish, Arthur, one only you can fulfil.' And before he'd been able to say anything else, she'd stood on tiptoe and replaced her finger with her mouth. Her lips had been trembling, tasting of sugary desire with a hint of sweet desperation. He'd known she'd had a crush on him and he'd been flattered. Then she'd kissed him, and he should have put his hands on her shoulders and gently eased her back…but he hadn't.

In that one moment, he'd become intoxicated by her… and had kissed her back. He'd had to force himself to take his time, to be gentle and not rush into a hard and hungry kiss, which was exactly what he'd wanted to do. He'd cupped her face with his hands and cherished her mouth, delighting in every response she gave him. When he'd pulled back, both of them breathless, he'd looked into her eyes and would never forget the mixture of surprise, trepidation, confusion and the smallest hint of fear he'd seen there.

Surprise. Trepidation. Confusion.

Surprise, trepidation, confusion…and fear! That was exactly how Maybelle had looked at him that evening.

Arthur sat bolt upright in bed, belatedly realising he'd been dreaming. His heart was thumping erratically against his chest as he held onto that last thought.

Surprise, trepidation, confusion and fear. Maybelle had looked at him in exactly the same way May had looked at him all those years ago, although Maybelle's ratio of fear had been much greater. It didn't matter that her eye colour was different—it was the *look*.

His eyes widened as his brain seemed to be reaching far-fetched connections. May and Maybelle. Maybelle and May. May*belle*. His beautiful May!

He'd known there was something familiar about Maybelle Freebourne…but was it possible? Was it true? Were Maybelle and May one and the same?

CHAPTER FOUR

MAYBELLE WAS AT work early the following morning. What was the point of lying in her bed, marking time, when she could be doing something useful? As it turned out, when she arrived just after five o'clock, the ED was packed and the night staff were grateful for her help.

She'd spent half the night with her thoughts tumbling one over the other as she'd tried to figure out what she should do. Should she cut and run right now? Leave Victory Hospital and get a job somewhere else? Or work at the hospital but find a new place to live? That was the problem with being in witness protection, she was so used to change it was second nature to her, yet she wasn't used to settling down. There was no permanence, no ability to remain in one place because as soon as a threat came, their entire family had been uprooted and moved yet again.

The big question was, if she stayed, would she be able to work alongside Arthur and still maintain her equilibrium? She'd certainly failed last night but if she kept her professional mask in place whilst at work and avoided him when at home, then surely she'd be able to see out her twelve-month contract. Besides, she really wanted to work at this hospital. It was nostalgic and with the recent death of her father it was helping her to focus on happier times.

Should she let a little thing like a past relationship with the man who had been like a big brother to her get in the way?

Arthur was far more than a big brother, her heart stated, but she pushed the thought away. She couldn't think of him in such a way because if she did, it would derail everything she was trying to do. Romantic entanglements were the last thing she needed when trying to carve a new life for herself.

With new determination, she continued on with her work, treating her patients and saving lives. When the handover from the night shift to the day shift had finished, Maybelle could feel her anxiety starting to rise. Arthur would be here soon. He'd probably want to talk to her, demand an explanation, and she wasn't sure she wanted to give him one. Lying to people wasn't something she enjoyed and in the past she'd had to lie in order to protect herself and her parents.

'Except the threat is over,' she reminded herself softly. That only made things worse because now she was lying to protect herself only. Maybelle eased back and looked at the ceiling, trying to figure out how her life had become so incredibly complicated in such a short space of time. She heard a sound behind her and spun around so fast in her chair she almost gave herself whiplash. Was it Arthur? She held her breath as she came face to face with Gemma.

'Morning.' Gemma looked bleary-eyed and half-asleep. 'Need coffee,' she mumbled and headed off to the kitchenette. Maybelle continued with her work until the next little noise startled her. It was ridiculous because with every little sound her heart rate would increase and then decrease when she discovered it wasn't him. Where was he? Wasn't he rostered on today? She'd simply presumed that, as Director, he'd be around during the day but she didn't see him until the afternoon.

Eight-year-old twin girls had been brought in by ambulance, one suffering from abdominal pains and the other having sympathy pains.

'It's worse for me,' Evie told her twin, who was clutching her abdomen in pain. 'There's nothing wrong with you, Lizzy.'

'But it hurts!' Lizzy's tone was filled with anguish.

'Lizzy does have a temperature,' Cici reported as she finished doing Lizzy's observations.

'Evie's abdomen is excessively tender,' Maybelle said after she'd palpated the girl's stomach. The anxious parents were waiting in the corner of the room, both looking whiter than their girls.

'They were premature,' their mother stated. 'They were in the children's hospital in Melbourne for the first three months of their lives and any time either one of them is sick, I tend to crumble.'

'When both of them are sick, like this, it takes us back to that time when they were so small and unwell,' their father added, doing his best to reassure his wife.

'I'd like to scan the abdominal area of both girls, as pain can manifest itself in different ways. We'll give them both some pain relief because even psychological pain can be quite debilitating,' Maybelle told the parents.

'This isn't the first time something like this has happened,' their father added. 'When Lizzy was four, she sprained her wrist and Evie was the one in pain.'

'We just like doing things together,' Evie clarified, listening to the entire conversation while her sister sweated and moaned with pain. Cici was trying to sponge the girl down, needing to break the temperature.

'Let's get some analgesics into them and then we can run some tests.' Maybelle wrote up the notes for the required medication.

'What could it be?' The mother's anxiety was starting to rise. 'What's wrong with them?'

'I won't be one hundred percent sure until I have the results from the ultrasound,' Maybelle said. 'But possibly appendicitis.'

Lizzy moaned at this news. 'Appendix. Is that scary?'

Maybelle smiled and headed to Lizzy's side while Cici did Evie's observations again. 'A lot of things are scary when you come to hospital,' she told a very concerned Lizzy. 'In fact, when I was about your age, I was admitted to this same emergency department with appendicitis.'

'Were you?' The question came from a deep voice behind her. Maybelle knew that voice far too well and she quickly looked over her shoulder to see Arthur standing just inside the curtain, listening to what was going on. 'You came to Victory Hospital to have your appendix out?' he continued, shaking hands with both the parents and quickly introducing himself. He scanned Evie's and Lizzy's charts just as quickly and as thoroughly as he scanned Maybelle's face. Did he think she was lying? That she was offering a false story in order to keep the girls nice and calm?

'That's a coincidence. I had a friend who had her appendix out at this hospital when she was eight years old as well,' he said, then waggled his eyebrows at Evie. 'Clearly you've come to the right hospital because we know how to deal with appendicitis.' He checked both girls and confirmed the assessment. After Maybelle had administered the analgesics, the girls were wheeled to Radiology for their ultrasounds.

How could he have remembered she'd had appendicitis as a child? He hadn't even visited her in hospital, although Clara had been there every day after school. Perhaps it wasn't her he was talking about. Perhaps he'd had another friend who'd had their appendix out when they were eight. That was a definite possibility. Wasn't it?

Now all she needed to do was to keep her distance from Arthur. He was at the nurses' station, chatting with Gemma about something, but she could have sworn he'd glanced in her direction several times. It was odd how she could almost feel his gaze on her, checking to see where she was, as though he was about to confront her, about to reveal her secret in front of everyone, to strip her defences bare.

When he'd finished talking to Gemma he headed down the corridor to his office and Maybelle breathed a sigh of relief. Given how she'd left his apartment last night, she was feeling more jittery than normal and tried hard to control her rising anxiety.

'Any more patients I need to see?' she asked Gemma. She needed to be doing something, anything.

'I think we're good right at the moment. Why don't you go and have a cuppa?'

Maybelle shook her head. The prospect of bumping into Arthur in the kitchenette was too high. 'I'm good. Is there anything else I can help you with?'

Gemma gave her a quizzical look, but then shrugged and handed her an inventory list on a clipboard. 'Some of the treatment rooms are running low on stock. I was going to go and get it later—'

Before Gemma had finished speaking Maybelle had taken the clipboard from her.

'Glad to help.'

'OK.' Gemma was clearly surprised at a doctor volunteering to do a task usually performed by orderlies, nursing or clerical staff. 'There's a stock trolley just over there. If you can get everything on the list, then I'll get Cici to re-stock the rooms when she has a moment.'

Maybelle nodded before heading off to collect the stock trolley. The stockroom was most definitely a good place to hide from Arthur, plus she'd be helping Gemma.

'You just need to keep out of his way,' she mumbled to herself as she tried three times to swipe her pass card through the sensor. Finally, the door opened and she headed into the small room with the stock trolley and list of required items. The door clicked shut behind her and she breathed a sigh of relief. A reprieve…for now, but she couldn't spend the next twelve months running away and hiding from Arthur.

As she started to find the contents of the list and arrange them on the stock trolley, Maybelle's thoughts began to churn. How on earth was she supposed to keep her distance from him when he seemed to be near her at every turn? At work. At home. Perhaps finding somewhere different to live would be the best option. That seemed good. At least then she'd be able to have some time to relax and not be on constant 'Arthur' alert.

She didn't want to leave the hospital as she felt in her heart that this was where she was meant to be. Surely she could work alongside Arthur without him discovering the truth? If she simply kept denying they knew each other, he'd let the subject drop…wouldn't he? And, besides, what was the worst that could happen? What if he *did* discover who she really was? It wasn't as though her life was still in danger.

'Work through the scenario,' she told herself as she continued pulling supplies off the shelves and adding them to the trolley. 'If he finds out, then you simply tell him the basic details of the matter and notify the case worker that Arthur knows the truth.' She continued to take calm, reassuring breaths.

Besides, even though she'd made a bit of a mess of

things last night, Arthur probably thought she was some sort of crazy woman and hadn't given it another thought. Perhaps all he cared about was her doing her job so he could keep the ED running smoothly. Wasn't that what was important?

When she'd finished filling the trolley, she tried to open the door but found it locked. There was a swipe access panel next to the door and she belatedly realised she needed to swipe her card to get in and out of the room. She swiped her pass card but the door didn't open. She tried again several times but the door remained firmly locked.

'Seriously?' she grumbled as she pulled her cellphone from her pocket but after a moment realised there was no cellphone reception in the small room. Frustrated and annoyed, Maybelle accepted there was nothing else she could do except wait. At least Gemma knew where she was and when someone finally said, 'Where's Maybelle?' they would come looking for her.

While she waited, Maybelle tidied the already tidy shelves simply because she needed something to do. She wasn't the type of person who was good at sitting and waiting, but once the shelves were as neat as they could possibly be there was nothing else for her to do except wait and try swiping her access card every thirty seconds.

She was almost at the point of complete and utter boredom when the sound of the door clicking open made her heart jump for joy. It then skipped a beat altogether when Arthur came into the room.

'Sorry it took me so long to realise you were missing,' he remarked.

'It's only been...' She checked her watch, more for something to do than actually checking the time because in actual fact she knew exactly how long she'd been waiting to be rescued. 'Twenty-two minutes.' Maybelle grabbed the end of the supply trolley and went to wheel it out, only then realising that Arthur had shut the door behind him, effectively locking them both in.

'Why did you shut the—?'

'I didn't mean just now,' he interrupted.

There was something in his tone that forced her to lift her gaze to meet his, rising anxiety starting to pulse through her veins.

'Er…well…erm…what do you mean?'

'You've been missing for twenty years…May.'

'Uh…' She forced a tight-lipped smile and shook her head. He'd figured it out and there was nowhere for her to run and hide. How had he figured it out? What should she say to him? She decided the best course of action was to maintain her cover story. 'It's Maybelle.'

'Why did you run out of my apartment last night?' Straight to the point. That was so like him.

'I don't think this is the right place to discuss such a topic,' she said, standing opposite him, both of them with their backs to supply shelves. He was dressed in trousers, white shirt, college tie and his usual white doctor's coat. His hair was a little mussed, as though he'd been raking his hands through the soft locks in frustration or agitation. His grey eyes were looking at her with such intensity that she was positive her heart skipped a beat. Good heavens, did the man realise just how utterly gorgeous he was?

'I think it's the perfect place because there's no escaping.' He paused for a moment as though trying to collect his thoughts. 'Even if I've got this wrong, I just need you to hear me out. Please?'

At her hesitant nod, he began. 'Ever since you walked into the ED yesterday morning, there's been something niggling in the back of my mind. You're so incredibly familiar to me, Maybelle, and then last night…watching you eat and the way you smiled when you cuddled Juzzy and how your eyes widened when I spoke about Clara and then seeing you so upset when you were looking at that photograph…' Arthur raked both hands through his hair, an action she'd seen him do several times when he'd been exasperated. 'Who are you?'

'Maybelle Freebourne.' Her words were soft.

'Why did you cry when you saw that photo? If you're not May Fleming then you at least must know her. What happened to her?'

'What makes you think—?'

'Just stop.' He held up both hands. 'I'm not going crazy. You know something, and for some far-fetched reason you can't tell me. Are you being threatened? Are you unsafe?'

'Arthur…' She paused, trying to think of what to say next.

'Even the way you say my name, especially like that, is familiar. I know you…and I also know there's only one way to prove my hypothesis.'

With that, he took a step towards her. What was he doing? Was he going to…to kiss her?

Maybelle immediately put up her hands to protect herself but all that did was make them come into contact with his shirt-covered chest. Her fingers tingled with heat, a heat that spread up her arms and flooded her entire body. How was it that this man could affect her in such a way? That he could make her heart race, take her breath away? Cause her to be filled with need and desire and all with a simple glance?

When he raised a hand to cup her cheek she gasped with repressed need. 'Wait.' The word was a whisper. 'Wh-what are you doing?' Her tongue came out to lick her dry lips and she watched as he watched the action, his Adam's apple sliding up and down his smooth throat as he swallowed.

'I'm going to kiss you.'

At the soft, deep words Maybelle's entire body was ignited into a frenzy of longing, one she hadn't felt in a very long time.

'Why?'

He was very close now, his head already starting to dip towards her own, his gaze flicking between her eyes and her lips but lingering on the latter as though he needed this just as much as she did. 'Because it's the only way to be completely sure you are who I think you are.'

She opened her mouth to ask another question but instead had her lips captured by his, her breath catching in the moment. There was definitely no denying anything now because, as her eyes closed, it was as though she was transported back to the moment of their first kiss...in the backyard of his parents' house at her sixteenth birthday party. Back then, she'd been determined to seize the moment, to let Arthur know that she didn't think of him as a big brother any more but rather as someone who had stolen her teenage heart.

To her utter astonishment and complete delight, he had kissed her back. Kissed her tenderly, testing and teasing, just as he was doing now. How was it possible that his scent was still so intoxicating? Or that the taste of him was exactly the same, except with more knowledge and experience in the background?

When he eased back, they both exhaled, their breaths mingling. She stood with her eyes closed, trying to grasp the magnitude of what had just happened. Not only was it now impossible to deny exactly who she was, but worse than that was the realisation that whatever had been brewing between herself and Arthur two decades ago still lingered in the far recesses of their minds and bodies.

He slid his fingers down from her cheek to cup her chin, his thumb brushing lightly over her still-parted lips. 'May?' Her real name was a question on his lips. 'It's you.'

Maybelle looked at him from beneath hooded lids. 'Yeah.'

'What…? How?' He dropped his hand and took a step back, shoving both his hands into his trouser pockets. 'Why are you called Maybelle?'

She exhaled slowly, trying to get her breathing to return to normal so she could make some sort of attempt to explain the past two decades in the simplest way possible. Even then, she had no doubt he'd want to know the ins and outs of exactly what had transpired. She knew she would, if the positions were reversed.

'When we left—'

'When you and your parents vanished without even a simple goodbye,' he interrupted, a hint of old annoyance in his tone.

'We were put into witness protection.' The words seemed to tumble out of her mouth in a rush.

He was silent for a moment as he processed this information. 'OK.'

'OK?'

'OK.' He shrugged. 'Clearly something bad had happened and it was necessary to protect your family from harm and it explains your sudden disappearance without a word of warning.' He nodded again. 'OK.'

'Just like that? You accept what I'm saying?'

'After that kiss, there's no reason for you to lie to me.'

'I…guess not.'

'So your name is Maybelle now?'

She was still trying to process the fact that Arthur had

simply accepted her explanation with no other questions or repercussions. Where were the twenty questions? The need to understand the details of exactly what had happened with her parents, of the threat they'd all lived under for far too long? 'Yes. It's as close as I could get to my real name.'

'And Freebourne?'

'I chose Freebourne because, technically, I'm free from the threat.'

'You've been reborn?'

She smiled as he pulled out his pass card and swiped it through the access panel, the door clicking open on the first try.

'Something like that.' He was holding the door open and grabbing hold of the stocked trolley before Maybelle held up her hand to stop him. 'Wait a second.'

'What?'

'That's it? That's the extent of the explanation you need to let you know that you're not crazy? That I'm the same person you grew up with? The person who vanished from your life without a trace?' Especially after what had happened between them the final night before she'd left?

'A lot of things finally make sense,' he said with a shrug of his shoulders. 'May...belle.' This time when he spoke her name his gaze rested momentarily on her lips before he smiled. 'It suits you. A sort of grown-up version of May...and you've definitely grown up.' He winked at her then, just like he had in the past, just like he had yesterday when he'd been teasing her, but this time, the wink was filled with a double entendre. Then he turned on his heel and wheeled the trolley from the supply room, leaving a stunned Maybelle to follow him.

She'd been so used to playing her cards close to her chest, not confiding anything about her true identity to anyone, and now that she had, Maybelle couldn't help but experience a sense of anticlimactic confusion. She was happy Arthur had believed her so readily, that after their shared kiss he knew there was no way she could lie to him.

Perhaps this new life of hers wasn't going to be as difficult as she'd originally thought…except, of course, for the fact that her attraction to Arthur was most definitely still there after all these years. What she was going to do about that, she had no clue. No clue whatsoever.

CHAPTER FIVE

NOW THAT SHE wasn't hiding the truth from Arthur, Maybelle couldn't believe how free and giddy she felt. It was almost as though she were happily intoxicated because she didn't need to lie to him any more. Free. She felt free and freedom had been the one thing she'd been craving for years.

When the twins, Evie and Lizzy, returned from having their scans, Maybelle looked at the results on the computer screen. 'Evie definitely does have appendicitis,' she confirmed, explaining to the girls' parents what would happen next. Arthur was standing beside her as she spoke, which made her feel a little self-conscious. Yes, he was her boss and he had every right to monitor her when she spoke to parents and patients. However, this didn't feel like a test but more like a 'let's work together' type of thing...and Maybelle liked it.

'We've called the surgical registrars, who will be down very soon to take Evie to Theatre. They'll be the ones to go over the consent forms with you.'

'And Lizzy?' their mother asked.

'Lizzy is fine, just sympathy pains.'

'She's not faking it, you know.' The protective maternal tone was insistent.

'Oh, no. I completely agree and to that end I'll be prescribing some fast-acting analgesics to help take away Lizzy's pain until Evie's out of Theatre and on the mend. There have been a lot of research papers written about emotional pain transference with twins and sometimes with close siblings who aren't twins. I'd also like to admit Lizzy tonight because once Evie's out of Theatre, it will aid in Evie's recovery if Lizzy is close.'

'If everything progresses well,' Arthur added, 'the girls should be able to go home tomorrow afternoon or early the following morning.'

'That's right. Our ED clerk is organising beds for the girls in the ward but with the advances in technology and the means of removing the appendix via laparoscope, the surgery is much easier nowadays.'

'Better than when you had your appendix out?' the dozing Evie asked, rousing for a moment.

Maybelle smiled and placed a hand on Evie's forehead, brushing a few strands of hair out of the way. 'Much better,' she confirmed.

'And here's Felicity. She'll be the doctor looking after you,' Arthur said, introducing the surgical registrar to the girls and their parents. Once the handover was complete, the girls were transferred to the surgical ward, where their treatment would continue.

'Another satisfied customer,' Maybelle said, as she sat at the desk and started typing her notes onto the computer. Arthur looked at the list of patients waiting to be seen but kept glancing over at Maybelle. 'What is it?' she finally asked.

'Huh?'

'You keep looking at me as though you're—'

'Seeing a ghost?' he interrupted.

Maybelle glared at him. 'You said you didn't need any

explanations.' Her words were quiet and she looked around to make sure no one could overhear their conversation.

'It's not an explanation I'm after, per se, but...' Arthur leaned in closer and stared into her eyes. 'Why are your eyes brown? You used to have the bluest of blue eyes.'

'Contact lenses.' Maybelle tried to ease away because when he'd leaned closer to her she'd caught a breath of his hypnotic scent and found it difficult to look away from his own sexy eyes. He'd grown into an extremely handsome man and she was stunned he wasn't yet married. No sooner had the thought come than she voiced it. 'Why aren't you married?'

'I was. Now I'm divorced. Didn't work out and right now I'm more than happy to do the work and career thing.'

'Oh. I'm sorry it didn't work out for you.'

The corner of his lips twitched. 'Are you?'

Her heart skipped a beat when he looked at her like that and with his sexy scent still winding its way through her senses, causing a flood of awareness and desire, Maybelle slowly shook her head from side to side. 'As long as you're happy.'

'You, too.'

'I hope the two of you are discussing a patient.' Gemma's words interrupted their *tête-à-tête*. 'Because if you're not, there's some serious sexy stuff going on between you.'

Arthur's answer was to laugh, turning to face the clerk. 'You think there's serious sexy stuff going on between everyone.'

Gemma joined in the laughter. 'It's true. I do. What can I say?' She sighed longingly. 'I'm a hopeful romantic.'

Arthur left to go and see a patient and Maybelle watched, confused by what had just happened. She had definitely been drawn in by him, staring intently into his eyes as he'd stared into hers. Like Gemma, she'd thought there'd been some serious sexy stuff going on but apparently not. Did Arthur flirt like that with all women? Was this just part of his natural charm? Something she'd misinterpreted? He had kissed her, though. Had she misinterpreted that? Had he been interested in kissing *her* or had it simply been a way for him to prove he wasn't going insane?

Was that why he wasn't that curious as to what had happened to her? Hadn't he just stated he was more focused on his career than romantic entanglements? She shook her head, more cross with herself than with him. She'd been so worried about him finding out about who she really was that she hadn't considered how he would treat her once his curiosity had been satisfied.

This was why she did her best not to get personally involved with the people she worked with. She didn't need to be contemplating such questions when she was at work. It was unprofessional and, more importantly, she didn't like herself for being weak and letting Arthur get under her skin so easily. They'd known each other in the past—so what? They'd shared some kisses and highly intimate moments—so what? They'd kissed, less than two hours ago, in the supply room and it had been…breath-taking, mind-boggling and heart-stopping—so what?

Gritting her teeth, she shoved all personal thoughts of Arthur Lewis to the back of her mind and concentrated on her job: treating patients and writing up her notes.

When her shift was over, Maybelle walked the five blocks back to her apartment, rugged up against Melbourne's cold weather but pleased it wasn't raining.

As she showered her day away, she resolved to only think of Arthur as an old family friend and a new colleague. Nothing more. Once she was dressed in her pyjamas, she sat down and made a list of all the things she still needed to purchase. At the moment she had the basics when it came to furniture, such as a table and four chairs, a bed, a wardrobe and a lounge suite. She would, however, like a microwave and a blender.

She also needed to lease a car. It was the most direct way of getting transport because right now she didn't have the time it took to purchase a good car. Maybelle was just looking up the number for a car leasing company when she heard a dog yapping outside her door. Intrigued, she opened her apartment door and, sure enough, there was Fuzzy-Juzzy sitting proudly. Behind her stood Arthur with a bag of take-away food in one hand and a bottle of wine in the other.

'Dinner?' he asked with a smile, and before she could reply, Juzzy ran past her into the apartment.

'Juzzy!' Maybelle called, and quickly chased after the dog. Spending another evening with Arthur hadn't been on her agenda so if she could quickly catch the dog, she could politely refuse him. 'Juzzy, come here.' The dog was sniffing her way around the apartment and just when Maybelle thought she had the pooch cornered, the dog would dart to another location.

Finally, Maybelle was able to pick the dog up but by the time she'd done that Arthur was in her kitchen, already dishing up the food. The dog was licking her and nuzzling with delight, clearly happy to be with her. So, it appeared, was Arthur.

'I'm starving. I hope you like Italian cuisine.' He placed the plates on the table with cutlery then hunted around the kitchen for a pair of wine glasses. Eventually, he pulled out two coffee mugs. 'No wine glasses, eh? Looks like you need to go shopping.' He tapped the list she'd made. 'I'm free on Saturday and so are you.'

'How do you know when I'm free?'

'Because I draw up the rosters. I'll come by around ten o'clock. It's always good to have a sleep-in when you can.'

Maybelle stood, still holding Juzzy and patting the dog, who was snuggling into her as though they were the oldest of friends. She shook her head. 'What are you doing, Arthur?'

'Pouring wine into coffee mugs,' he replied, before carrying the wine-filled mugs to the table.

'I mean what are you doing here, providing me with dinner—again?'

He looked at her for a long minute before shrugging. 'You need to eat and so do I. We've had a long day—'

'You have questions.' It was a statement and for some reason Maybelle was disappointed.

'Don't you? We've got twenty years of catching up to do.' Arthur pulled a clean dog bowl from one of the bags he'd brought in and opened a can of dog food for Juzzy. Sniffing, the dog scrambled to be free of Maybelle's arms and headed into the kitchen, where Arthur was most definitely making himself at home.

Once Juzzy was eating her dinner, Arthur walked behind Maybelle and held a chair for her, indicating she should sit down. Realising it was easier to accept than refuse his nice gesture, Maybelle sat down and waited until Arthur was seated.

'Thank you. For dinner, I mean.'

'Welcome.' He peered at her. 'You haven't taken your contacts out.'

'I don't usually do that until I go to bed. Besides, the contacts are also prescription so taking them out means finding my glasses and at the moment I think they're at the bottom of a packed box.'

'What happens when you wear the glasses out and people see that you have blue eyes instead of brown?'

'Simple. I don't wear my glasses out of the house. In fact, it's very rare I wear them at all.'

'But what if friends drop by unannounced?'

'And bring dinner and their dog with them?' Her words were pointed.

'Exactly.'

'I don't have friends who drop by.'

'Never?' Arthur started eating the delicious spaghetti Bolognese he'd brought.

'When you're in witness protection it's best if you don't make friends, at least not ones who feel comfortable enough to drop around unannounced.' She twirled a forkful of pasta before raising it to her lips and chewing, belatedly realising just how hungry she was. 'Mmm… This is delicious.'

'Good.' He was looking at her with a slight frown creasing his forehead, a hint of sadness in his eyes. To have spent years keeping herself distant from others, from not making any real friends…he couldn't fathom it. 'I've also brought you one of their take-away menus.'

'Thank you. That's so kind.' She gestured to the food. 'This is kind, too. You're still a kind man, Arthur.'

'Thank you. However, I think I've changed quite a bit in twenty years, as, clearly, have you.' He put down his fork and raised his coffee mug to her. 'A toast.' He waited while she followed suit. 'To learning more about who we are today.'

'Why? Why would you want to do that?' When she made no move to bring her cup towards his, he clinked his cup to hers and then drank, sealing the toast.

'Why would I want to get to know you?' Arthur seemed surprised at the question. 'Because you're family,' he stated, as though it was the only logical answer.

'Family?' She quickly lowered her cup to the table as

a lump formed in her throat, the emotions of sadness and loss surprising her with their sudden appearance. 'I don't have family any more.' The words were out before she could stop them.

Arthur put his fork down and reached out to place his hand over hers. 'Your parents?'

The warmth of his touch, combined with the caring compassion in his tone, caused her to feel vulnerable. She shook her head, biting her lip in order to get the surge of sadness under control. 'Mum's been gone just over ten years now and Dad died four months ago.'

'Oh, Maybelle.' He shifted his chair around the small round table so he could be nearer to her. The next thing he did was to envelop her in his arms, drawing her closer. 'You're on your own? Is that why you've come back to this district? To a place where you felt comfortable?'

'Yes, exactly.' She'd forgotten what it was like to have someone comfort her and while she wanted to accept that comfort more than anything in the world, the ingrained training to keep her distance rose to the fore. She stiffened her spine, hoping to send the signal that she didn't like being touched in such a way, but either Arthur didn't pick up on it or ignored it completely. More than likely it was the latter. It reminded her that being in his arms, resting her head against his chest, feeling the heat from his body infuse into her own had made her feel so safe and secure. 'How could you possibly know that?'

'Because that's exactly what I would have done in your place.' Arthur watched as Maybelle tried to contain her emotions. It only took a minute and she was back under control. He couldn't imagine what she'd been through but the difference from the young teenage girl to this deeply controlled woman was vast. He dropped his arms and returned his attention to his food.

It was clear she didn't want to talk about things too much and he was fine with listening to whatever she wanted to share and curbing his curiosity about what she didn't want to say. Besides, his instinct to draw her into his arms, to offer comfort had been a huge mistake because now her fresh scent was lodged in his senses, enticing him to want more. The kiss they'd shared in the stockroom still lingered on his lips, begging him to repeat the action again and again.

Even at the nurses' station, when he'd been looking deeply into her brown eyes, the need to kiss her had been intense and he'd forced himself to walk away, to put some distance between himself and this woman…this woman who could turn his world upside down with one simple smile.

Maybelle Freebourne was even more dangerous to his thoughts than May Fleming had been. Back then, he'd been an adolescent intrigued and bewitched by her. Now he was a grown man with more life experience and more willpower, yet here she was, bewitching him all over again. She was as dangerous to his thoughts as ever. Since he'd kissed her, he hadn't been able to get her out of his mind. Like a moth to a flame, he'd ordered them dinner, using poor Juzzy as a diversion to gain access to her apartment. Desperate measures. That's what he'd employed. Desperate measures in order to spend more time with her, to be with her, to breathe her in, to see if that spark he'd felt when he'd kissed her in the stockroom had been real or residual.

'What *can* you tell me, about the witness protection, I mean?' The question was necessary. He wanted to know and secretly hoped that she wanted to tell him, to open up to him, to share with him.

Maybelle ate another mouthful, chewing slowly as she

considered his question. When she spoke, it was as though she was choosing her words very carefully. 'My parents were scientists,' she started.

'Yes. I remember them working long hours in the lab and often forgetting they even had a daughter. Wasn't that why you spent so much time at our house? Some weeks you were there for dinner every night.'

She smiled at the memory. 'Yes. They were a little absent-minded and back then it did bother me that we weren't a "normal" family.' She laughed without humour at the words. 'Anyway, remember how we sort of wondered if they'd cured cancer?'

'You mean they did?' Arthur was astonished. If that was what had happened, why wasn't her parents' discovery celebrated? Why had they needed to go into witness protection?

'No, or not that I know of. My dad's speciality was the human genome and my mother—'

'Was into synthetic compounds,' he finished.

'You remember?'

He fixed her with a look, one that said that she shouldn't underestimate his intelligence. 'I spent a lot of time with you over the years and especially in those last few months, May…belle.' She smiled at the way he'd connected her old name with her new name, and the action almost made him lose his train of thought, such was the power her smile still seemed to have over him. 'I remember what your parents did.'

'OK, then. Well, even though their individual research was in two different fields, they often used each other as sounding boards. Eventually that meant that their research…' she linked her hands together '…combined, in probably the most scientifically interesting and yet earth-shattering way.'

'What was it? I remember you saying, just before you vanished, that your parents had been arguing more than usual.'

'And that was because they knew what they'd stumbled on.'

'Can you tell me what it was?'

'I can tell you the gist of it. As a safety measure, I wasn't allowed to be privy to their work, even after I'd obtained my medical degree.'

'So…in a nutshell?'

Maybelle sighed and actually leaned forward, closer to him, her voice dropping to a level just above a whisper. 'They developed a synthetic compound that was originally supposed to attack the genetic mutation for bowel cancer but ended up becoming a silent killer.'

Arthur's eyes widened at her words. 'In what form?'

'An injection of a minute amount could cause human death within seconds, leaving no trace of the synthetic compound upon autopsy.'

Arthur was stunned. It took a moment for him to wrap his head around what she was saying—and not saying. 'Nothing?'

'Nothing, and, believe me, even after we went into witness protection their work continued, but this time, instead of being funded by a pharmaceutical company with connections to underground cell organisations, they were funded by the government. As long as they continued to work for the government, we could remain in witness protection.'

'So it was still a restricted life.'

'A very restricted life—for them.'

'And for you?'

'I was able to get a medical degree, even though I had to change medical schools twice.'

'It was that bad?'

Maybelle closed her eyes for a moment, the food before her forgotten. 'Yes.' There was deep-seated pain in the word and when she opened her eyes he saw despair and hopelessness before they were quickly veiled. Anyone who had just met Maybelle Freebourne wouldn't think twice about such a look but he hadn't just met her. In fact, he knew her far better than she probably realised. He remembered everything about those few wonderful months they'd spent together, cuddling and kissing and talking. It was as though their souls had entwined in a way that even time and desperation could not separate. The realisation left him feeling a little shaken, especially as after his divorce he'd sworn off permanent relationships.

'We don't have to talk about it any more, Maybelle,' he offered. He didn't want her to feel despair and hopelessness any more. 'The last time I saw you, your hair was flying into the breeze as you raced from my house to yours.'

'You watched me?'

He nodded. 'From my window, through the branches of the tree. Once you'd climbed the fence into your yard you disappeared from view, but then…just as you reached the top of your balcony, I caught the most fleeting glimpse of you as you went over the railing and into your bedroom.' He put his thumbs and forefingers together, making a sort of rectangle shape. 'It was only the slightest glimpse and back then I had no idea that would be the last time I would see you—until yesterday.'

'I wanted to contact you, but…I didn't know what to say.'

'Clara told me that you sent her birthday cards.'

Maybelle nodded. 'It was easier to lie to Clara. I didn't want to but I could say to her that my dad had been transferred and she wouldn't have asked any questions.' She slipped her hand across the table and, to his surprise, laced her fingers with his. 'I didn't know what to write to you. I started several drafts but after what I said to you that night…' She paused, almost waiting for him to say something, and when he didn't she continued. 'You *do* remember what I said?'

'Uh…yeah. It's a little difficult to forget.'

She smiled at his words but then the smile slowly slipped from her face. 'That was the day the government entered our lives. The agents were downstairs, talking to my parents, when I came to see you.'

'What? Why didn't you tell me?'

'I didn't know what was going to happen next.' Maybelle slipped her hand from his. She could hear the confusion in his tone, the slight hint of censure because she hadn't told him *why* she'd behaved the way she had. 'All I wanted right then and there was to escape from my life.' She stood from the table and started to pace the room, agitated from talking about it. 'The way I felt about you was so…encompassing and I thought if I could lose myself in you, even for a short while, I'd find some level of happiness, of contentment. I don't know if I've ever been content.'

She paused, then angled her head to the side. 'Except for when I was in your arms. That was when I could dream, when I could imagine myself a different sort of life, a life where my parents were normal, where we could tell our families we were together and not have to sneak about.' Where they were grown-ups, in love with each other and wanting to spend the rest of their lives together. She bit back those last words because that clearly hadn't happened.

Arthur was silent for a moment, clearly processing her words. 'So I guess that explains why you demanded I make love to you.'

'I'm sorry, Arthur. It was an adolescent mistake to put you on the spot like that but—'

'Maybelle.' He stood and walked to her side, hearing the break in her voice, seeing the tears shimmering beneath the surface.

'I never meant to hurt you and I never meant to hurt me either because, believe me, I was hurting.' The words were a whisper and Arthur gazed into her upturned face for what seemed an eternity before drawing her closer, their foreheads resting together as they absorbed the truth of that lost night all those years ago.

'If only I'd realised…'

'Would you have said yes?' As she spoke the words, they were peppered with small hiccups as she tried to choke her emotions back where they belonged. It was only with this man that her vulnerabilities rose to the surface. Usually, she prided herself on staying in control.

'I would have held onto you and never let you go.' His voice was laced with a strong possessive streak and her heart leapt at the thought of just how much she'd meant to him back then. But what did she mean to him now? Was this…this thing between them simply residual? She pushed the question aside.

'We were just kids, Arthur. We'd been secretly dating for all of nine weeks.'

'Ten, actually.'

She was pleased to find his memory so precise. 'What could you have possibly done?'

'I don't know, but I would have at least *tried*.'

'Besides, even if I'd stayed, I'm not sure things would have lasted. You would have left home, gone to medical school. I still had two years left at high school and goodness knows what Clara would have thought of our relationship.'

'She was happy about it.'

'She knew?' Maybelle pulled back to look at him, delighted at the small twitch at the corner of his mouth as he smiled.

'She figured it out.'

'How? We were so careful.'

'So we thought.' He rested his hands at her waist, needing to keep her close. 'For the first four weeks after you left…well, let's just say I was a little dark.' He knew it had been longer than four weeks that he'd been angry at her but she didn't need to know that.

'A little dark, eh?'

'Or, as Clara termed it, in a permanent black mood.'

'Oh.'

'When she pressed me on the matter, I sort of blurted out that we'd been seeing each other. She gloated and kept saying over and over that she knew it, until I threw her out of my room.' He chuckled as he spoke, the sound floating over her like a welcome safety blanket. She liked it when he was happy. She liked his smile, the way his eyes twinkled, the way his lips twitched with mirth. Oh, those lips. Those lips had kissed her time and time again and she'd loved every moment of it. His thumbs were moving in tiny circles, rubbing at her waist, each stroke causing sparkles of desire to flood throughout her entire body.

Being this close to his delicious scent was making her want to breathe it in for ever, to resurrect the easygoing plans she'd had for her life all those years ago. At sixteen, she'd planned to finish high school, go to medical school and to marry Arthur. That's all she'd ever wanted.

'I wanted to say yes.' At his soft words, she raised her gaze from staring at his mouth to meet his eyes. 'That night. I wanted to say yes more than anything but I didn't want you to have regrets.' He lifted his head so he could look into her eyes, his clever fingers still creating havoc with her senses. '*I* didn't want to have regrets. Now we *both* have regrets.' It was his turn to stare at her mouth, indicating they were both on the same wavelength. 'I can't imagine what you've been through.' He wrapped his arms about her waist, drawing her closer against his body. 'I wish I could have saved you.'

And those words were her undoing. For years, that was all she'd wanted. She'd wanted Arthur to track her down, to come riding towards her on a white horse, her knight in shining armour, her King Arthur. In the end she'd had to learn how to save herself, but at what cost?

'Arthur…' She closed her eyes, unable to look at him any longer, unable to see the certainty reflected in his gaze. She swallowed, her throat thick with repressed tears.

'Hmm…?'

'Don't.'

'Don't what?'

'Be nice. Caring. Compassionate.' She bit her lip in an effort to bite back the rising tide of emotions she'd kept locked away for far too many years. Only with Arthur was she ever this vulnerable and it appeared time and experience hadn't changed a thing.

'Why not?' There was confusion in his tone as he tenderly brushed the backs of his fingers across her cheek, tucking a stray curl behind her ear. 'If there's one person in the world who deserves my compassion and understanding, it's *you.*'

And those were the words that broke the dam of emotion she'd been holding at bay for far too long, and before she knew it she'd burst into tears.

CHAPTER SIX

SHE WAS CRYING. She was crying and Arthur was comforting her. He was holding her close as she leaned her head against his shoulder and cried. She never cried. She'd become as hard as nails and she never cried...at least, not in front of anyone.

'We need you to be brave,' her mother had told her a lot during that first year in witness protection.

'She's strong. Far stronger than we realise,' her father had countered. 'Our girl understands the gravity of the situation.' He'd tapped the side of his head twice to indicate his daughter had intelligence. 'You won't catch this one breaking down at the drop of a hat.'

And she hadn't. She'd been able to control her emotions, to quash her fears, to hide her feelings. Maybelle had found herself in some terrible situations over the years and she'd coped with them all...and now, with one small modicum of compassion from Arthur, she was a mess.

Why was it that when someone did something nice, especially if the intention was genuine, it was so difficult to accept? And how incredibly wonderful did it feel to lean on him, even if it was just for a moment. In that one split second, all the wishes and dreams she'd had as a young girl came flooding back. All she'd ever wanted had been for someone to look out for her. Not in a protective detail kind of way but rather in an emotional 'I care about you' way. Her parents hadn't been able to provide her with that sort of care, as they'd been too busy providing it for each other. Then, after her mother's death, she'd had to be the one to care for her father as he hadn't known how to go on without the love of his life. How Maybelle had longed for such a love, for a man to be devoted to her in such a way... And with the way Arthur was holding her right now, it felt as though that sort of love might be possible, might one day become a reality.

The thought both frightened and filled her with questions. Was the person she'd become too different from the young woman Arthur had known? Was he still infatuated with the idea of them together or could he see the reality of their present situation—two people drawn together through the emotions of a mutual past love?

'Everything's going to be all right, Maybelle,' Arthur murmured, bringing her thoughts back to the present. The tears were starting to diminish and she became more conscious of the way Arthur was rubbing a hand up and down her back, soothing her.

'Is it?' She sniffed and eased back. He didn't try to hold her close to keep her captive and she was grateful. If he'd been anyone else, if he was a man she'd recently met, she'd be suspicious about his actions, but not with Arthur.

Free from his arms, she dragged in several breaths, trying to get her mind out of mush mode and back into logical mode. 'Is everything going to be all right?' She started pacing around the apartment, shaking her head. 'Because I have no idea if it is or if it isn't. Besides, isn't that just a token statement? "It'll be all right."' She used air quotes as she spoke. 'When people say that, what do they really mean?'

Arthur watched as she stopped moving and planted her

hands on her hips. Her eyes were flashing with determination, her tone was laced with stubbornness and her body language indicated she was spoiling for a fight. Good heavens, the woman was stunning!

'*Is* everything going to be all right, Arthur? Define *everything.* Do you mean politics? World peace? Are you talking about sport, wondering if your football team is going to win? Or perhaps you're referring to a patient, hoping they'll make it through their treatment?' She spread her arms wide, staring at him as though daring him to answer. She was toned, fit and healthy. That was all he could think about as she started pacing again, once more jumping up onto her soap box to continue her rant. All the while, all he could think about was how he desperately wanted to kiss her, and not just any kiss but a *real* kiss.

Yes, he'd kissed her at the hospital in the stockroom, but that had been to prove a point, to confirm he wasn't going crazy. What he hadn't expected was to discover in that stockroom that the attraction which had existed between them all those years ago appeared to have been on a low simmer, the fire never really having gone out. It was still there, still very much alive, and after that kiss it had been re-ignited with a vengeance. At least, it had been for him.

How did she feel about it? He'd already lived through a one-sided relationship, with his ex-wife deciding that monogamy wasn't for her. Yvette's affairs and her blasé attitude to her marriage vows had made him wary of other women. Yvette had loved him, had been interested in him, in sharing a life with him. She just hadn't understood why she also couldn't share a life with other men, be interested in other men and love other men.

His fiery red-headed defence attorney had plunged her hand into his body and ripped his heart out. Then she'd crushed it into tiny pieces and left it to rot. It had taken him almost eight years to piece his life back together, to try not to fixate on a woman's ulterior motive when they started dating.

And here he was, wondering how Maybelle had felt about that kiss in the stockroom? About how she'd felt when he'd held her close just now? About why she was ranting and raving the way she was? Was it all designed to put him off? To make him realise that she was a woman with a lot of baggage to sort out? The real question was, did he want to stick around and help her, especially when he wasn't sure he'd ever understand what it was she'd been through?

As she continued to pace and talk, he couldn't help but become aware of her fluid movements, how she seemed to glide with ease yet every muscle in her body was taut and on red alert. Was that how she'd lived her life these past years? On red alert? Never being able to fully relax?

He could hear his mother's words as she'd given him some advice he'd often employed. 'Sometimes, Arthur, you'll have to accept that you can't understand everything in life. Much like men and childbirth. They can empathise but they'll never truly know what it's like to give birth.'

He was facing that situation now. He could never understand but he didn't need to. What he needed was to find a way to ease Maybelle's constant pacing, her nervousness, her anxiety. Instead of getting lost in his own thoughts, he focused more closely on what she was saying.

'Yes, the threat is over. That's what I've been told ever since Dad passed away. With the death of my parents, the major threat has been removed. Now I've been "released back into society", whatever that's supposed to mean, and I'm meant to just lead a normal life?' Her voice choked slightly at the end and his heart turned over with sympathy. Arthur also knew that was the last emotion she'd want from him.

Maybelle stopped pacing. 'It's like a war hero coming back from being on tour, having witnessed distressing events, then being told to get back to the life they'd left behind. It's not that easy, especially when the last time I had a normal life I was sixteen years old.'

Listening to her, watching her movements, sensing her frustration, Arthur's need to help and protect her increased. He wanted to do all he could to help her settle into the normal life it appeared she was looking for. And yet the memory of the kiss they'd shared was still fresh in his mind and that brought another set of problems to the fore.

Could he open himself up to sharing his life with a woman? There was already the high probability that she'd hurt him again. Heavens, the last time she'd left, it had been as though she *had* ripped out his heart and taken it to wherever it was she'd disappeared to.

So just how far was he willing to go to help Maybelle find her new level of normal? He was attracted to her, yes, but was he emotionally capable of opening himself up to the possibility of getting hurt again?

'I don't know how to make sense of this new life, Arthur.' He looked across at her, meeting her gaze and noticing how emotionally helpless she looked. She *was* emotionally helpless and he was emotionally cautious. Not a wise combination. Could they find a safe combination? Could they go back to being friends and ignoring the effects of the re-ignited fire that surrounded them?

'I guess that's what I'm trying to say,' she continued when he didn't say anything. 'My life has been structured one way for so long—a life with strict rules and regulations because those rules and regulations were designed to save my life, which they did on several occasions.' Maybelle fluffed her curly blonde hair with her fingers and he had to admit the style really did suit her. Yes. He was definitely attracted to her. There was no doubt about that but could he be her friend? She didn't need any more complications in life and neither did he.

'But can I live my new life with rules that aren't as strict? Or rules that I have to make up myself? I need to put parameters in place but first I need to figure out what those parameters are.' She frowned and spread her arms wide. 'Am I making any sense?'

'Uh-huh.'

She fixed him with a glare. 'Have you even been listening to me, Arthur?'

'Yes. I've heard every word.'

'And yet with the way you're staring at me now, it's as though you'd like to sweep me off my feet and head towards the bedroom.'

Damn. Was he that obvious? Even hearing her say those words out loud caused a wave of desire to surge through him. He closed his eyes for a brief moment, trying to school his features into an impassive mask. Meeting her again had definitely disrupted his life and destroyed a lot of the preconceived ideas and theories he'd had regarding her disappearance. She was alive. She was healthy—emotionally scarred, but healthy. These were good things, given the alternatives, but what she needed from him now, and also what he needed from her, was some time to let the dust settle as they reconnected.

'I won't deny I find you attractive.' He kept his eyes closed as he spoke those words out loud, knowing if he looked at her it would make them all the more difficult to say. 'However...' Arthur dragged in a calming breath and finally opened his eyes. 'I want to help you, Maybelle.'

'How?' The question was quiet.

'By being your friend. I'm still processing the fact you're alive, and you're still figuring out your life. Any romantic entanglements are only going to complicate things and, quite frankly, I've had my fair share of complicated.'

'Friends?' She sounded sceptical.

'We've been friends before.' He smiled at her. 'Surely we can do it again.' It would require a lot of self-restraint from him but the choice was simple. If he pushed for a romantic entanglement, it might fizzle out within a month and then they'd start avoiding each other. As they worked together, and now lived very close to each other, that would cause more tension than he was willing to endure.

Besides, by a stroke of luck, she was back in his life once more. His old childhood friend. Wasn't that more important than any desire-filled tryst that would cause them both more pain? Maybelle was back in his life and he wanted her to stay there. The decision was cut and dried, so why did he feel as though he was lying to himself?

'Friends.' She sighed with relief. What did that sigh mean? That she didn't want a physical relationship with him? That she, too, had had enough of relationships that only brought stress and confusion? He halted his thoughts and watched as a lovely smile lit her features. 'Yes. We can be friends. Friends is good.'

'Excellent.' After resolving what had clearly been an undercurrent both of them had been avoiding, Maybelle sat down on the carpet, as though her body had no more energy to keep her standing upright. She crossed her legs and her head sank forward, only to be disturbed a moment later when a cute Fuzzy-Juzzy came over to her and started licking her hand.

Maybelle's unreserved laughter caused his gut to tighten. Good heavens, that was a glorious sound and as he watched her play with the dog, a smile of utter delight on her face, he wondered if he hadn't made a mistake. Just friends? It was going to take a lot of self-control for him to keep his promise.

For the next few days, Arthur made sure he kept to his promise of being friends with Maybelle. He helped her to lease a car—she'd refused to buy, saying she wasn't ready for that level of permanence yet—and provided her with a plethora of menus from take-away places that delivered.

'We could even do something completely wild and go grocery shopping so you have actual food in your apartment,' he'd suggested when he'd found her eating breakfast at the hospital cafeteria on Friday morning. He'd taken his coffee to her table and sat down, enjoying the surprise of spending some one-on-one time with her. The ED had been hectic during the day and he'd forced himself to keep his distance in the evenings. Surprisingly, he'd missed her. Missed seeing that smile that lit her features, or that little frown that crinkled her forehead, or the way she twirled her hair around her finger.

'Perhaps on the weekend,' she'd offered as she'd finished off her scrambled eggs, toast and coffee.

'You do realise the weekend is tomorrow?'

She paused for a moment. 'Huh. So it is.'

'Are you still planning to buy some extra bits and pieces for your apartment?'

'Yes. I need a microwave and a proper coffee machine.'

'And some throw cushions for your lounge and a few pictures to hang on the walls. Plus, didn't you say that your doona wasn't warm enough?'

'Yes—yes, I did. Right. I'll add doona to the list, but I don't think the other things are necessary.'

'Why not?'

'They're not practical, Arthur.'

'I beg to differ. Your lounge is incredibly uncomfortable, and a throw cushion might just make all the difference.'

'It is not uncomfortable.'

'Then why do you sit on the floor so much?' When she opened her mouth to protest, he leaned forward and pressed a finger to her lips. 'You asked me to help you find a normal life, Maybelle. Normal people have…'

He faltered as the warmth of her breath caressed his fingertip, the sensation travelling up his arm and engulfing him with desire. He swallowed and jerked his hand back, forcing the rest of his sentence out and hopefully covering over his slip-up.

'They have throw cushions and pictures on the walls.' Why had he touched her? Touching her provoked sensations he was desperately trying to keep under control and made them rise up to the surface.

'If…if normal people do it, then I guess I have to as well.' The sigh she gave was an exaggerated one but he hadn't missed the slight stumble over her words, indicating she'd felt that same natural chemistry that seemed to flow through them no matter how much they tried to deny it.

'We could definitely go shopping tomorrow.' As he said the words, the hospital cellphone on his belt started ringing. 'Uh-oh.'

'The phone of doom is ringing.' She started to pack up her dishes onto a tray so she could stack it on the dirty dishes trolley on the way out of the cafeteria.

He smiled at her words and was glad they'd worked their way past the dangerous moment. As he answered the phone, he made a mental note not to touch her again because it seemed the instant they made contact both of them lost all resolve over their self-control. At least, that was the way it was for him. He wasn't quite sure how May-belle felt about it.

They headed back to the ED, Arthur talking to Gemma on the phone.

'Let me guess,' Maybelle remarked once he'd ended the conversation. 'Emergency? Ambulances on their way?' Her words were laced with an easygoing sarcasm as she stated the obvious. Light-hearted banter. He could defi-nitely cope better with this light-hearted banter than being in close proximity where her sunshine-and-roses scent infiltrated his senses and made his need for her increase.

He laughed. 'See? This is why we only employ the best doctors in the ED. They're so switched on.' They worked together in Emergency, treating their patients and sta-bilising them so they could be transferred to either the ward, the emergency theatres or back home. That evening, Arthur decided it was time he tackled the mound of paper-work that was starting to swamp his desk. He gathered the new stack of papers Gemma had handed him and started towards his office.

'Are you working on those at home tonight?' Maybelle asked as she fell into step beside him.

'That was the plan.'

'Need any help? I could order pizza. Halve the work-load.'

It was a tempting offer. To sit and talk about boring work stuff with someone who completely understood what he was on about, both of them eating pizza and making the mundane chore less of a chore, would be wonderful and it was for that very reason why he had to decline her offer.

'Thanks, but it shouldn't take me too long.' He went to use the pass card for his office door but it failed twice. He was balancing a mound of papers in a rather precari-ous fashion and if his stupid door didn't open soon, he was going to end up dropping everything. Add to that the fact that Maybelle's delightful summery scent was winding itself around him, driving him crazy, and it was little wonder he was starting to get a tad impatient.

'Here. Let me,' she said as she took the pass card off him and swiped it through the sensor at a different angle. The door clicked and Arthur immediately entered his office, almost tripping over his own feet in the rush to put a bit more distance between them.

He dumped the papers onto his desk and shook his head. 'And they said we'd be living in a paperless office by now. Sheesh!'

'So is that a yes to help and pizza?'

'Actually, I think I might just knuckle down here and get it done. You can, however, help me by feeding Juzzy.'

'Oh. Uh…sure.'

He could see she was disappointed. Did she want to spend time with him because she liked being with him? Or perhaps she simply didn't want to be alone? Or worse yet—she liked doing paperwork? 'Great. I'll get my spare keys for you.' He opened the small safe that was located in a cupboard under his desk and took out a set of keys.

'You keep spare keys at your office?'

'Where else would I keep them if I accidentally locked myself out?'

'Huh.' She accepted the keys. 'So that's what normal people do.' She tapped the side of her head as though making a mental note.

'What would you have done if you'd been locked out of your apartment? You know, in the "not so normal" world of witness protection?'

'I would have asked my bodyguard if I could borrow their key, or get them to break down the door,' she stated, then shrugged when he stared at her. 'There's not a lot of immediate privacy when it comes to witness protection. Someone always has to know your whereabouts.'

'Was it always that way?' He couldn't help the question. He didn't want to dwell on the past or bring up bad memories for her but at times his curiosity got the better of him.

'For the first year, definitely. Then things settled down for a bit.' She paused, looking off into the distance. 'It changed again when my mum died, that's when I had a bodyguard for a while, but…' Maybelle drew in a breath and forced a polite smile. 'All over now.' She jingled his keys and repeated his instructions for Juzzy to make sure she had them correct. The last thing she wanted to do was to overfeed his dog.

After she'd left, Arthur sat down in his chair and reflected on the newest snippet he'd learned about Maybelle. He really couldn't comprehend what she'd been through in any way, shape or form and yet here she was, trying to make a new life for herself…on her own. She really was… the most amazing woman he'd ever met.

Maybelle felt very strange walking into Arthur's apartment without him being there. Then again, the only other time she'd been here she'd felt just as strange. She turned on the light and quickly closed the door behind her as Fuzzy-Juzzy started barking and running in her direction. The dog almost stopped short when she realised it wasn't Arthur walking through the door but after a moment seemed to be pleased someone had come to feed her.

She trotted to the laundry where her food bowl stood empty. She even tapped the bowl with her nose as though to give clear direction of exactly what she was wanting. Maybelle couldn't help but laugh at the dog's antics and dutifully gave her food as per Arthur's instructions.

When the dog started eating, Maybelle crouched down and stroked the soft fur.

'You really are gorgeous,' she told the dog, who didn't miss a bite. It only increased the longing for a pet of her own but she wasn't sure if she was ready for *that* level of normal. What if there was another threat? What if she needed to move? She wouldn't be able to take the animal with her and that sort of heartbreak was one that could be avoided. For now, though, she could spend a bit of time with Juzzy and let herself dream.

She sat down on the floor and waited until the dog had finished eating, delighting in watching the Pomeranian's every move with her curly little tail and twitchy little nose. What stunned her further was when the dog decided to climb onto Maybelle's lap and seat herself there.

'This isn't your bed,' Maybelle told the dog, but she didn't seem to care.

She raised her head to look at Maybelle as if to say, *I'll sleep where I want, thank you very much, and I choose here.*

Maybelle stroked the soft fur and rested her head back against the cupboard, her legs stretched out in front of her. She could get used to this, having someone accept her and love her unconditionally, just as Juzzy was. There were no questions, no censure, no recommendations on what she should do with her life. There was just…love, and Maybelle absorbed it.

She continued to rhythmically stroke the dog, the action proving far more relaxing than she'd anticipated. Given she was sitting in Arthur's apartment, stroking Arthur's dog, she couldn't help but ponder whether Arthur would be like Juzzy, able to accept her unconditionally. She knew she was broken, damaged and even a little shell-shocked, and that she had a long way to go before she could really let herself relax, but it was possible, wasn't it? She *would* get to her goal in the end, wouldn't she?

For so many years she'd told herself that happy endings weren't for everyone and she was one of the people who was missing out. Sitting here, stroking Juzzy's fur and relaxing—far more than she could ever remember before—Maybelle began to let the faintest glimmer of hope start to ignite. It *was* possible. Why shouldn't she have a happily-ever-after ending? Hadn't she been through enough already?

Not only had her life been uprooted at the age of sixteen, she'd had to watch her mother die in the most horrific way possible. Then, recently, her heart had broken as she'd seen the utter despair and regret in her father's eyes not long before he'd given up the fight.

Although she'd felt alone for so many years, she now was truly alone. Being in witness protection had bonded her family together even more, which only made the loss of her parents even greater.

Closing her eyes, Maybelle continued to draw comfort from Juzzy's warmth as she stroked the dog. For so long she'd wanted nothing more than to be out of witness protection but now that she was, it was incredibly scary. She was facing her future all alone, and it was that loneliness that made a few tears slide down her cheeks. Sniffing, she wiped them away, annoyed at herself for not controlling her thoughts better.

These past few days with Arthur had been wonderful. Yes, the beginning had been a bit rocky but now that he knew her true identity, and seemed happy she was back in his life, the two of them had managed to rekindle their friendship. Naturally, it was different from how it had been all those years ago as they'd both had different experiences

that had moulded them into who they were today, but the
essentials of their friendship seemed to have remained.
Arthur had told her that she was like family to him and
even early today he'd mentioned the possibility of taking
her to see his parents.

'They'd be delighted to see you again.'

'But…how do I tell them who I really am?'

'You just tell them, Maybelle.' He'd shrugged as though
he wasn't sure what her problem was.

'It's not that easy, Arthur. For far too long I've had to
hide who I really was. I had to change my name, my hair,
my eye colour.'

'Was the threat really that bad?'

'That *bad*?' Tears had welled in her eyes and she'd been
far too aware that they had been at the nurses' station, in
the middle of the ED. Shaking her head and doing her best
to get her emotions under control, she'd swallowed and
said in a vehement whisper, 'My mother was murdered. In
front of me.' With that, she'd excused herself and headed
to the women's changing rooms in an attempt to get herself under control.

The next time she'd seen him had been just before she'd
left work, when he'd been carrying all those files to his office. Her offer of help had been rejected and she couldn't
help but feel that Arthur was already putting distance between them. If she hadn't told him about her mother, they
might well be sitting here now, enjoying pizza, laughing
together as they managed to sort out the ridiculous amount
of paperwork that was attached to the administration of
a department.

Arthur had wanted time away from her. Away from
her because she was far from a normal woman. She was
emotionally scarred—and she hadn't even told him that

the instant her mother had been killed she'd been drugged and held to ransom for the next two and a half days. Although it had happened ten years ago, she still had nightmares about it, often waking up thinking someone was after her, trying to kidnap her again.

'That's all in the past. That's all in the past. That's all in the past.' She spoke the words over and over again, trying to calm her mind, forcing herself to focus on the rhythmic movements of stroking the dog, concentrating on how the soft fur felt against her fingers, of how she seemed to be patting Juzzy in a pattern. Two strokes one way, a touch under first one ear, then the other, then several long strokes down Juzzy's body.

As though Juzzy wanted to reassure her, the little tongue licked Maybelle's hand, tickling her and making her smile. It helped the constriction in her chest to ease and her breathing to even out. Juzzy's body became heavier, the licks now few and far between as the dog settled into a secure and comfortable sleep.

She followed suit, her hand slowing in its movements, but the dog didn't seem to mind. Finally, she rested her hand on the dog's back, both of them content within the long moment that seemed to stretch into an eternity.

'Maybelle?' Her name was like a caress on Arthur's lips and she could have sworn she felt his hand on her shoulder. She tried to open her eyes but they were just too heavy. Her hand automatically started to stroke the dog's soft coat again but stopped after two short strokes, exhaustion claiming her.

'Hmm?' She felt herself warmly enveloped in his big strong arms, being held firmly as he picked her up and carried her. Then she was placed on a comfortable bed, one with a nice warm doona that seemed to cocoon her, lock-

ing out the bad dreams, the fear and trepidation that had
hounded her life in the past. 'Safe,' she whispered, then
turned her head into the pillow and slept.

CHAPTER SEVEN

ARTHUR WENT INTO the kitchen and checked on Juzzy, unsure how he felt at having Maybelle so close. Where he hadn't wanted to spend time with her, doing paperwork and eating pizza, because he simply hadn't been able to trust himself not to grab her and kiss her, he now had to fight the way she'd felt in his arms, the way her scent seemed to be permanently swirling around him, confusing his logical thought process.

Since she'd made a reappearance in his life, his thoughts had been continually drifting back to the past, pleased he now had some answers to the questions that had sat at the back of his mind for far too long. They may not have been the answers he'd been expecting, especially the bombshell she'd dropped earlier today, telling him that her mother had been murdered.

He'd always had mixed feelings about Maybelle's parents but most of them were from an adolescent perspective. He'd thought they should have paid more attention to their daughter, that they should have spent more time with her, but now, as an adult and as a medical professional, he could understand their dedication to their profession. Add to that everything Maybelle had told him about their work and he had a new appreciation for Samantha and Hank Fleming. To think of Samantha being killed and then to think of Maybelle witnessing that incident—his heart ached for them both.

In fact, it had made it almost impossible for him to concentrate on his paperwork and in the end he'd given up and left the hospital early, wondering if he could drop by Maybelle's apartment and offer her a hug. He wanted her to know he was there for her, as a friend, as a sounding board, as a guide in finally obtaining the normal life she wanted. He doubted, given what she'd told him, that her life would ever be completely normal, but then a lot of people in the world managed to make it through very traumatic experiences to achieve a *new* level of normal. That was what he wanted to help Maybelle to achieve. After all, deep down inside she was still his May and she was still most definitely beautiful.

What Arthur hadn't expected was to find Maybelle sitting on his laundry floor, the dog on her lap, both of them asleep. How long had she been there, sleeping in such an awkward position? When he'd moved the dog from her lap, he'd expected Maybelle to stir, but she hadn't. That was when he'd realised just how exhausted she must be. Had she been sleeping at all since moving to town? She'd said that her father had died a few months ago, so had she managed to have a decent night's sleep since then? This entire week she'd been at the hospital long before her shift began, which usually indicated the inability to sleep or settle.

With Juzzy all tucked up in her little bed and sleeping soundly—just like Maybelle—he made himself a cup of tea and took it to his bedroom, pausing momentarily outside the door where Maybelle slept. Should he check on her again? Was that creepy? What if she woke up and didn't know where she was? Perhaps he should leave her a little note, telling her not to panic?

He closed his eyes and shook his head, continuing on

to his own bedroom and shutting the door firmly behind him. Even the sight of her cocooned beneath the doona, snuggled deep and murmuring the word 'safe', had been enough of an undoing for him for one night. The need to hold her close, just as he used to, to talk quietly with her, just as they used to, to offer his support and to listen to what she had to say, was becoming more intense with each passing second he spent in her company.

Instead, Arthur forced himself to get ready for bed, deciding that tonight it might be advantageous for him to sleep in pyjama bottoms and an old T-shirt...just in case of an emergency or in case Maybelle sleepwalked or—

His thoughts stalled on the fact that she might very well sleepwalk. Sleepwalking was often attributed to stress and anxiety, the subconscious attempting to deal with what the conscious found difficult, and Maybelle had definitely had her fair share of anxiety and stress. What would he do if she sleepwalked right into his bedroom? He swallowed at that thought and sat back on his bed, resting against the headboard. He could well remember the last time she'd been in his bedroom, although that time she'd come through the half-open window rather than using the door. He'd been studying for an exam and although it had been late, he'd only managed to get through half of his notes. Then she'd appeared.

The memories that he'd locked away so many years ago came flooding back as he recalled the events of that night. The window had been right next to a large tree, one he'd climbed up and down several times over the years. The screen from his window had long since been removed to make covert access to his room easy when he'd arrived home past curfew.

The cool summer breeze had brought welcome relief from the oppressive heat they'd been enduring, but the last thing he'd expected to come through his window that night had been the girl who had been constantly in his thoughts for the past few months. Ever since they'd kissed at her birthday party, Arthur had found it difficult not to think about her, not to want to kiss her again and again and again…and to his dismay he had. They'd shared inviting looks across the dinner table while the rest of his family had been eating dinner; they'd allowed their fingers to touch when doing the dishes together; they'd sneaked kisses when no one had been around. And then she'd appeared in his bedroom.

Drawing in a long, deep breath, it was as though the smells of that night were re-creating themselves around him now. She'd been dressed in light sandshoes, three-quarter-length summer jeans and a light blue T-shirt. Her hair had been loose, the long strawberry-blonde locks floating around her shoulders, enticing him to reach out and run his fingers through them. It was her eyes, though, her bright blue eyes that had reflected her emotions of eager, wild, urgent desire.

'May!' He'd placed a hand over his heart at her sudden appearance, although even now he wasn't sure if he'd been startled by her or desperate with desire for her. 'What are you doing?' He'd stood from his desk and drunk his fill of her.

She hadn't given him an answer, except to walk purposefully towards him, wrap her hands around his neck and pull his head down so their lips could meet. The action had been done as one fluid movement and the grip she'd had on his neck had been tight, as though she was never going to let him go. Her lips had been demanding, insistent, desperate.

For a brief second he'd kissed her back, because how could he not? She was warm and inviting and tasted like strawberries mixed with pure sunshine. Intoxicating and addictive, he'd wanted more, he'd wanted everything she could give, to greedily have his fill of her. The hunger inside him had been met and matched by her, something she'd never done before, and a part of him had been delighted at this turn of events…but the reasonable part of his brain had begun to make itself known, begun to question why she was there, why she was kissing him in such a fashion and why she was manoeuvring them towards the bed.

Finally, he'd come to his senses and put his hands on her shoulders and eased her firmly from him. 'What…?' He'd swallowed, slightly breathless and captivated by the sight of her. 'What's going on? What are you doing here?' He'd glanced towards the door, afraid that his parents or his sister might walk into his room and find her here. Yes, it had been late. Yes, his parents had retired to bed, but still, the fact that he'd had a girl in his room at such an hour had been something that had made him feel skittish.

'I want you, Arthur.' Her words had been firm, with no hint of hesitation, and as she'd spoken she'd made a move to kiss him once again.

'Whoa. Wait a second.' He'd dropped his hands from her shoulders and taken a few steps away, needing to put some distance between them. 'What's going on?' He'd tried again, hoping this time to get some sort of sensible answer from her.

She'd shrugged her perfectly sculpted shoulders and had started to twirl one finger in her hair, a sure sign that she'd been nervous. 'We've been sneaking around for a while now, stealing kisses here and there, talking on the phone and having some very unsuccessful tutoring sessions.' She'd smiled at him then and he couldn't help but return her smile as he'd recalled the two of them sitting at the kitchen table while he'd tutored her in mathematics. His father had been at work and his mother had taken Clara to her violin lesson, which had left the two of them alone for twenty minutes. They'd made good use of the time, enjoying a make-out session rather than an algebra session.

'That still doesn't explain why you've sneaked out of your house and into my room.'

'And here I thought the words "I want you, Arthur" would be all the explanation you required.' With that, she'd made her way to his side and started kissing him again, her sweet lips enticing him to give in to the powerful urges he'd been desperately trying to fight. This time, though, they had been much closer to the bed than before and when she'd eased herself down to sit on the mattress, he'd been too captivated to resist following.

His fingers had tangled in her hair and his mouth had matched the intensity of hers. She'd smelled so good, as though she'd just had a shower and blow-dried her hair. The strands had been as soft as silk and touching them had only added fuel to the fire already raging inside him. He'd wanted her. There had been no question of that. For the past two and a half months he'd become increasingly infatuated with her, so much so that he'd been considering throwing all caution to the wind and suggesting they tell his sister and their parents they were dating.

It had been her idea to keep their burgeoning relationship a secret from everyone. Initially he'd understood her reticence with their parents, but Clara had been her best friend and he hadn't wanted to be the person to splinter that long-standing friendship. Having May in his room, in his arms, on his bed had meant that things had become far more serious much quicker than he'd anticipated and if anyone—family, friends, strangers—had asked him if he'd had strong, romantic feelings for her, there was no way he'd ever be able to deny it. In fact, he'd been positive that what he'd felt for her could also be defined as being in love.

He'd been so caught up in the heat, in the pheromones, in the realisation that this was really happening, that she was really in his room, really wanting him to make love with her, that he'd almost missed the slight hesitation as his hands had slipped to the waistband of her jeans. Almost.

'What's wrong?' he'd asked, breaking his mouth from hers and staring into her eyes. There, the hesitation had been confirmed and he'd quickly removed his hands, placing them back on her shoulders. 'We don't have to do this.'

'Yes. Yes, we do. I…I want to do this.'

'Honey, you don't need to do anything. I'm not going to force you.' He'd wanted to make that absolutely clear.

'Oh, I know you would never do that. Never.' The words had been adamant and he'd breathed a sigh of relief that she'd known he would never take advantage of her.

'Then why? Why come here and say what you did when you clearly have reservations?'

'Because I don't want to die a virgin!'

A loud crack, followed by a thud reverberated around him and Arthur sat up with a jolt. Had that sound come from his memories? He remembered being completely floored by her words back then, as though his entire world had ripped apart at the seams. Why did she think she was going to die? Why the sudden urgency? Yes, his thoughts had been turbulent at the time but right now he was unsettled. His gut told him something wasn't right and he always followed his gut instincts.

Arthur crept from his bed over to the door, opening it slowly before staring at the closed door to the spare room. Everything seemed quiet but the fact that Maybelle was here meant he was on edge. Was she all right? Should he check on her? Deciding it couldn't hurt to check, he walked from his room and reached out for the door handle. Before he could touch it, the door was wrenched open and he was whacked on the head with something hard.

'Ugh.' He instinctively raised a hand to ward off the next attack. The next thwack hit his arm and he realised her weapon of choice was a large hard-back dictionary. 'Maybelle. Maybelle. It's me.' His words were punctuated by a few more swipes of the book, which he managed to dodge. 'May!'

When he spoke her real name she paused, her breathing erratic, and from what he could see of her in the darkened room her eyes were wide and filled with confusion. The book was raised in her arms, ready for another strike. It didn't matter that his head hurt, it didn't matter that something had caused her to completely freak out. All that mattered was getting through to her that she was safe, that she wasn't in any danger—at least, not from him.

'It's Arthur.' He tried once more to calm her down and when she lowered the book, letting it drop to the floor, he stepped forward and placed his hands on her shoulders. 'You're safe, May. You're safe.'

'Arthur?' She looked up at him with utter confusion and the urge to resist her was lost as he gathered her close into his arms. She went willingly, wrapping her arms around his waist and resting her head against his chest. Arthur held her trembling body, doing everything he could to let her know she was safe.

He breathed in the scent of her hair, allowing the present-day reality to combine with his past memories. He'd held her like this on several occasions, especially that last evening. They'd been lying on his bed, above the covers, fully dressed, his arms around her, holding her, talking quietly with her.

'I love the sound of your heartbeat.' It was a few minutes later that she mumbled the words against his chest. 'I would often think of lying there in your arms, listening to the soothing *lub-dub* of your heart as you stroked my hair and spoke reassuringly in your deep, modulated tones.'

He smiled at that. 'Deep modulated tones?' He tried to ease away but she only tightened her grip around his waist, clearly not ready to break the hold.

'Your voice has a certain…cadence to it and I've always equated that with safety.' Only now did she slowly lift her head from his chest and look up at him. 'There were times in my life when things weren't safe, when we'd been discovered and had to leave everything in the middle of the night and try to start our lives again.'

'Oh, sweetheart.'

'And when my life was so uncertain, when I had no idea from one day to the next what was happening, where we were going to live, what my name was going to be…then I would remember that night. That special night…with you.'

'Nothing happened.' He wanted to make sure she was remembering it the right way.

'Everything happened, Arthur.'

He eased back and this time she let go. 'That's not the way I remember it.' He bent to pick up the book, wanting to put some distance between her and the item that had connected with his skull. Returning it to the shelf, he took her hand and led her from the room.

'Where are we going?' she asked, but thankfully didn't fight him.

'I'm making us some tea. You're clearly delusional.'

'A strong shot of whisky would probably help more but I'll take the tea.' And there it was, that wonderful, teasing sense of humour he'd missed so much. He glanced at her over his shoulder and smiled.

'I've missed you.' The words were out of his mouth before he could stop them and Maybelle squeezed his hand and nodded.

'I missed you, too.'

They stood and stared at each other for a long moment, the air around them almost starting to crackle with electric tension. It had always been this way, ever since that first kiss so very long ago. He glanced at her mouth—that perfectly sculpted mouth that had always fitted so perfectly with his own. Swallowing, he met her eyes and only now that they were in the artificially lit kitchen did he realise she'd removed the contacts.

Bright blue eyes, the colour of the sky on a cloudless summer's day, gazed back at him, repressed desire visible in their depths. She bit her lower lip and he realised she was nervous. He didn't blame her. He was nervous, too. He knew it was possible for the physical attraction he'd felt all those years ago to return with a forceful thump but the emotional connection, the one that years apart should have wrecked, was still very much alive.

Then, before he could think anything else, she'd moved towards him in one fluid motion, wrapped her hands around his neck and pulled his mouth down to meet hers. It was exactly that way she'd approached him all those years ago, as if she had to follow through on her desire before she lost her nerve.

Memories of the last time she'd done this and the fresh sensations of the present blurred together to make one almighty, powerful aphrodisiac. Where years ago the kiss had been testing and hesitant, this time it was filled with heat, experience and adult appreciation for the possible outcome such a kiss could evoke. Gone were the questions about whether or not they should consummate these feelings because this time there was no doubt that she wanted him and definitely no doubt that he wanted her. There was no hesitation, no hesitation at all.

How was it possible after all this time that the sweetness of her mouth was just as intoxicating? The woman was in his blood. That was the only explanation he could garner. She'd left an imprint that hadn't faded and now it was time to bring their story to the full conclusion.

'This needs to happen,' she whispered against his mouth. 'I've dreamt about it for so long.'

'You have?' The words were mumbled between them as he spread kisses across her cheek and down to her neck. She'd always liked it when he'd kissed her neck and now was no exception. Tilting her head to the side and allowing him access to her smooth, delicious skin, she moaned with delight before sliding her fingers into his hair and momentarily massaging his scalp. He liked that. He liked that she knew him and he knew her. When she tightened her grip on his hair and pulled his head up, he knew she was ready for the next onslaught of emotions, the heat between them now at a dangerous level.

This time when their mouths met there were no more questions, no more hesitation, no more confusion. Hot and hungry, they devoured each other, her hands sliding beneath the T-shirt he wore and making short work of removing it. The tantalising touch of her fingertips on his skin left a trail of desire-filled fire that only fuelled him on. She broke free from his mouth to smother his chest with kisses that nearly sent him over the edge. He groaned with longing, with need, with desire as she continued to create havoc with his senses.

'Do you have...*any* idea, what you...do to me?' he ground out, his hands at her waist, holding her body close to his.

'I think...you do the same to me,' she returned as she

lifted her own knit top over her head, revealing a lilac-coloured bra beneath. Before he had time to drink his fill, she'd pressed her almost naked chest against his and captured his lips with hers. 'I want you, Arthur,' she murmured against his mouth. 'Even more than I did back then.' She kissed him again and again and he accepted those kisses, but there was a pinging noise at the back of his mind that was gradually getting louder and louder.

'You do know we didn't...' He gasped as she nipped at his lower lip. 'We didn't do anything.'

'Not in my world.' Her words were fast and impatient as though she wanted things to continue on their natural course of progression. She eased back ever so slightly and grabbed both his hands in hers, urging him from the kitchen and back towards the bedroom. Arthur was too dazed, too stunned to believe this was actually happening, that they were going to rewrite history and actually—

'Wait.' He stopped her in the hallway just next to his open bedroom door. 'What do you mean, "not in my world"? We didn't have sex that night, Maybelle.'

'We should have.'

'We couldn't!'

'What does it matter now?' she said as she backed into his bedroom, beckoning him closer.

'It matters that whatever you're doing now, you're doing it for the right reasons, that you're not simply trying to live out a fantasy of a life you weren't able to have.'

'You're overthinking this.' She perched herself on the end of his bed and gazed at him with such devotion he almost capitulated.

'Am I?' If this was going to happen, he didn't want either of them to have regrets.

'I want you, Arthur. Isn't that reason enough?'

'And what about tomorrow? What about working together? Trying to be friends? Don't you think having sex will change all that?' He stayed in the hallway, trying to keep his logical thoughts in place, even though his libido was telling him otherwise.

She frowned at him for a moment, as though she was trying to process what it was he was actually saying. 'Are you turning me down *again*?' Maybelle spread her arms wide, glaring at him with those incredible eyes of hers. He had no idea what had happened to her brown contacts and he didn't care. All he cared about right now was the pain in her eyes and the fact that he'd been the one to cause it.

'I'm not saying we *shouldn't*, I'm just saying we should perhaps take things a little slower.'

Her grin turned wolfish. 'Slow is good.'

'Maybelle.' There was a slight warning in his tone and he leaned against the doorjamb. 'Is this what you really want?'

'Arthur, it's all I've wanted since I was sixteen. I want to know what it's like to be with you, to have you as close to me as humanly possible. I want to know what it's like to sleep in your arms all night long, to wake up with you in the morning, to sit together at the breakfast table and read the paper.'

He raised his eyebrows in surprise. 'You want marriage?'

'Marriage!' Her surprise echoed his. 'What? No. That's not what I meant.'

'So you *don't* want marriage?'

'Arthur…' She glanced around his room and spied an ironed shirt in the closet. She took it off the hanger and put it on, clearly feeling self-conscious standing in the middle of his room wearing only her trousers and bra. The problem was she looked even sexier wearing his too-large shirt. 'I don't know what I want. I don't know what's going on in my life. I don't even know who I am yet. The last thing I need is to drag anyone else into my upside-down world.'

'Yet you're clearly willing to drag me in…to a point.'

'You're different.'

'So you *do* want to drag me in?'

Maybelle sighed with impatience before closing her eyes and shaking her head. 'I'm saying I don't know what I want. No one ever knows what they want.'

'But you just told me that you wanted *me*.'

She opened her eyes and glared at him. 'That's not what I meant. Stop taking everything I say out of context. Yes, I want you—*physically*—but long term…?' She shrugged, her shoulders rising and falling in his too-big shirt. 'Do you? Do you know what you want?'

'Yes.'

She rolled her eyes. 'Of course you do. You're Arthur. You plan everything.' She paced around his room for a moment then fixed him with a glare. 'I've often wondered, back then, if it had been your idea to have a romantic tryst, then it would have happened. You would have pulled out all the stops in order to seduce me but the fact that *I* was the one who came to you, asking you to make love to me, well…there was simply no dice.'

'What? Maybelle, you were confused and young and—'

'Desperately in love with you,' she pointed out. 'And you were in love with me, or so you said.'

They'd been two very confused teenagers back then. He full of general teenage hormones and angst, and she full of confusion and fear. 'I couldn't take advantage of you, Maybelle. What if having sex had hurt you—physically? What if you'd become accidentally pregnant? What if you'd hated me for taking advantage?'

She sat down on his bed, twirling her hair absently with her finger as she pondered his words. The action only made her look more appealing and the fact that she was doing it unconsciously made his heart lurch for her. How was it that even after all these years, after everything they'd been through, she still looked innocent? 'I hadn't thought of it like that,' she said after a moment. 'I just presumed all teenage boys wanted to have sex.'

'They do. I did. I *really* did.' He wanted to venture into the room, to sit beside her, to put his arms around her, to hold her close, but he was shirtless and she was…well, she was adorably sexy and incredibly inviting. 'However, that night we had together was one of the best nights I've ever had. Sex is one thing but we had a connection. We bonded that night.' Arthur couldn't keep the passion from his tone. 'It was an amazing night.'

'It was.' She dropped her hand to her side and stared unseeingly at the room before her. 'I thought about that night often, usually when I was melancholy or upset. Memories of that night would cheer me up, would give me hope.' Hope that one day she'd bump into him again but, given her circumstances, she'd known it to be impossible. A small smile touched her lips. If only her past self could see her now, sitting on Arthur's bed, wearing one of Arthur's shirts, her lips still tingling from Arthur's kisses.

'A lot has happened in our lives since then,' he pointed out.

'Hence why you're suggesting we stick to being just friends?' Maybelle covered her face with her hands and he could tell she was feeling foolish. 'Yet I kept pushing, kept insisting, kept throwing myself at you in an effort to satisfy my own desires.'

Arthur gave in and crossed to her side, crouching down in front of her, pulling her hands from her face. 'I have those same desires, Maybelle.'

'Yet you clearly have more self-control than I do.'

'Perhaps that's because I know where I want my life to lead.'

'And where's that?'

'My career. My research. I put two grants in for funding and one was accepted last week.'

'Your *research*?' The way she said the word it was almost as though he'd just told her he wanted to stick a needle in her eye. 'That's all that's important to you? What, wouldn't you want to get married again? Have children?'

He shook his head and stood, walking away from her, unable to see that look in her eyes, the one that was silently calling him a traitor. 'Research is important. It can change people's lives, it can change the way surgeons perform various operations, and without research there would be no further advances in medical science.' He was on the defensive and he knew it.

'You're darned right when you say that research can change people's lives.' She shook her head and he couldn't blame her for feeling that way. With her parents being married to their research and, in the end, having that research affect her life in such a dramatic way, it was little wonder she was looking at him as though he was out of his mind.

'And with regard to marriage, it didn't work for me. I tried the house in the suburbs.'

'And children?'

'My ex-wife didn't want any.'

'And how about you?'

Arthur spread his arms wide. 'Of course I wanted to have children but it didn't happen.'

'What *did* happen, Arthur? Because, while you're very much the same as you ever were, this…' she pointed in the direction of his heart '…this part of you has always wanted

children. You told me so, remember? We were sitting on
the couch, making out instead of studying, and when we
both came up for air, you sat with me in your arms and we
talked about what we wanted for our future and you told
me you wanted to become a doctor, get married, live in a
house like the one we were in and raise children just the
way you and Clara were raised. You told me that, Arthur.'

It was true and he knew there was also no point in
lying to her because he'd nearly made the Freudian slip
of saying *their* house in the suburbs, *their* life together,
their children, because back then all he'd wanted was to
be with May Fleming for the rest of his life. That hadn't
happened. 'That was then.'

'What happened, Arthur? What happened with your
marriage?' Maybelle's words were filled with sadness and
regret for him. At least her disdain for his proposed research projects had decreased…for the moment. He sat
down on the floor beside the bed and shook his head.

'Yvette was an attorney—well, she still is. She prac-
tises in both Sydney and Los Angeles and is now a junior
partner in the firm.'

'Impressive. How did you meet?'

'I was being sued.' He shrugged his shoulders. 'A
wrongful action against the hospital I was working at.'

'In Melbourne?'

'Sydney,' he offered.

'You moved to Sydney.' She smiled with surprise and
shook her head. 'It's a wonder we didn't run into each other
sooner. I spent several years at Sydney General Hospital
and several in the outer suburbs.'

'Wasn't meant to be.'

'And you were married to Yvette the attorney. I'm
guessing it was good in the beginning?'

'As all marriages are.' He stretched his legs out in front

of him and leaned back on his hands. Maybelle shifted up the bed and rested her head on a few pillows, watching him, listening to him, her heart aching for the pain he'd endured. 'Yvette was dynamic and funny.'

'And beautiful.'

Arthur smiled at that. 'Naturally. She wasn't afraid to go after what she wanted—and at the time she wanted me. I was a doctor. For her, whenever she had to network with clients and other firms, having a doctor for a husband, being the epitome of a professional couple, was important to her.'

'But not for you.'

'No. I was more interested in spending time with *her*, getting to know *her*, wanting to be with *her*.'

'And she…'

'Wanted to spend time with her senior partner, in his bed. And with her colleagues, in their beds, and with other attorneys from other law firms, in their beds.'

'Oh, Arthur. I'm so sorry.'

He scoffed. 'She wasn't. She couldn't understand why I thought that *marriage* meant we couldn't see other people. She thought we had a great professional relationship. She never complained about how often I was at the hospital, about my dedication to my work, about my career plans. In fact, she told me she applauded them and that if we stayed married, she'd be able to assist me with the rise in my career, with networking, with playing the dutiful wife and hostess at business functions and conferences.'

'She *sounds* like an attorney.'

'She's a good lawyer. We had a house in the suburbs. She didn't want to buy it. I did and she ended up getting it in the divorce. We had two cars, mine was a normal sedan and hers was a sports car, and yet she ended up with both in the divorce.'

'But she was the one who'd committed adultery.' May-belle lifted one hand as though completely confused by what he was saying.

'I just wanted it to be over. I agreed to most things just so I could end it as painlessly as possible.'

'And yet it's left a lasting scar on your heart.'

'It has.'

'We all have our pain.'

'But mine is nothing compared to yours.' He sat up and shifted towards the bed, still remaining on the floor as though it was safer. It felt incredible to be talking to her again, to be sharing with her, to know that she was actually interested in what he had to say, even if she didn't always agree with it.

'Your pain is *your* pain. Don't compare it to mine.' She yawned as she spoke and closed her eyes.

'I want to stroke your hair,' he murmured, and she opened one eye to look at him. 'I'm only saying this out loud because I don't want to touch you when your eyes are closed and have you freak out on me again, breaking my hand because I've frightened you.'

Maybelle started to laugh as she recalled how she'd thumped him with that dictionary. 'I'm so sorry, Arthur, about hitting you with the book, I mean.'

'Where did you think you were?' He asked the question softly as he gently reached out to touch her blonde curls. He sifted his hands through the silken strands, knowing it was a mistake, that doing such a thing was not putting distance between them, but right now he didn't know how to stop himself.

'Locked in a room.'

'Why were you locked in?'

She closed her eyes. 'Because I'd been kidnapped.'

'You were kidnapped?'

Maybelle bit her tongue to try and get control over her rising emotions. Talking about the experience had never been easy and she usually avoided it as much as possible, but Arthur was asking and if she was going to tell anyone about the ordeal it was him. Her Arthur. Her protector. Her knight in shining armour.

'Uh… Mum and I had decided to go to a conference in Sydney. We were living in Broken Hill at the time, all three of us working at the base hospital there. I was just finishing up my internship and my parents were secluded in one of the research labs.'

'Still working for the government?'

'Yes, but in secret. They would work on their pet projects, my father still researching the human genome and my mother doing her work with synthetic compounds. That was the reason she'd wanted to go to the conference in Sydney. Part of her research had been handed on to a different scientist, who had taken it to the next level.'

'I take it your parents were never credited for their work?'

'No. That had been one of the conditions of witness protection. There were to be no unauthorised trips, no unauthorised research and no ownership of the research. At times it was difficult, more for my mother than my father, as she'd worked so hard, made so much progress and then, when the research was at a certain level, it was taken from her and handed on to another researcher, one who could work on it and publish the findings.'

'That would have been difficult.'

'And that was why she and I went on an unauthorised trip to Sydney. We thought we'd taken precautions, that we'd registered under pseudonyms, changed our hair and eye colour, everything we usually did, but this time we had no bodyguards, no one looking over our shoulders, no one telling us what to do.'

'And your dad?'

'He was against it at first but my mum was always able to talk him around and in the end he covered for us with the government.' Maybelle sighed, a small smile on her lips. 'We had a great time. Driving over to Sydney was fantastic. It was as though the veil of secrecy that had shrouded our lives for almost ten years was lifted and we could be ourselves. Samantha and her daughter May, taking a road trip together. Mother and daughter time.' She opened her eyes for a moment and looked at Arthur. 'That road trip to Sydney contains some of my favourite memories and I felt as though I was really getting to know my mum. Not as my mother—'

'But as a person in her own right,' he finished for her.

'Exactly.' The smile slowly slid from Maybelle's lips. 'The trip back, however, contains the worst memories of my life. You see, somehow Mum had been recognised at the conference. Even though we'd sat in the middle of the crowd, even though we didn't speak to anyone, even though we'd gone through all checks and precautions as we'd been taught. I don't know how they figured out who she was but it wasn't until we were between Cobar and Wilcannia—'

'Which means you were in the middle of nowhere,' he added.

'They…they started shooting at our car.' She paused, her heart starting to pound wildly against her chest, the images of what had happened flashing through her mind like snapshots. She clenched her eyes tightly shut, wanting to shut them out but unable to. 'We hadn't even realised we were being tailed. We were…we were having fun, laughing together, and then there was a loud bang and Mum found it difficult to control the car as it started swerving all over the place. Then the next thing I knew the car was rolling. Over and over.' She remembered screaming, of putting out her hands in order to try and brace herself, but the screams were muted, as though she was watching the picture unfold without sound. She'd caught a glimpse of her mother's face and noticed the terror.

'We…we came to a stop. The car was on its side and I managed to undo my seatbelt and climb out. I was about to go around to Mum's side of the car—she was lying with her head against the steering wheel, at such an odd angle—and then I felt arms clamp around me. I hadn't even realised there was anyone else there. They held me. Really tight. I tried to struggle against them, to remember everything I'd been taught by my case worker, but that all stopped as I saw them drag my mother's body from the car. She was still breathing. She was alive but unconscious.' Maybelle shook her head and sniffed. 'Then they put a cloth over my mouth and nose and…as things started to go black…as I began to slip into unconsciousness, I heard a gunshot.' Her words were broken and she sniffed again, trying to draw breath into her aching lungs.

She flinched back as Arthur's hand touched her face. Maybelle opened her eyes and glared at him.

'You're crying,' he murmured softly, and it was then she realised he was wiping away her tears with his thumb.

'I am?' She sniffed once more and immediately sat up. Arthur shifted back to give her some space, offering her a tissue. 'I'd better go.'

'No. Stay. I don't want you to be alone after reliving such a memory. Stay with me. I'll hold you. I'll make you feel safe. Nothing else will happen, I promise. Just…rest in my arms, Maybelle.'

She stood and took two steps towards the door. 'I would

like nothing more than to do that, but…I can't. I can't. I can't do this.'

And for the second time in a week Maybelle rushed from his apartment…and he simply let her go.

CHAPTER EIGHT

THE PICTURE OF him holding out his hand to her, offering support, to make her feel safe, especially with those hypnotic eyes of his, was difficult to get out of her head. Ever since she'd left his place in a rush, that picture had refused to disappear.

There was no doubt that a huge part of her had wanted to stay. Maybelle shifted on the lounge, resting her head back and closing her eyes tight. How was she supposed to get that image out of her mind? Arthur looking at her with devotion. Arthur looking at her as though he wanted nothing more than to really try and protect her for the rest of her life.

Was it possible? Would she be able to really put the past behind her and move forward? She shifted again, lying down on the lounge and wishing for a cushion to bury her face in as she remembered what she'd done to him. Shaking her head in embarrassment, she recalled attacking poor Arthur with a very heavy book. The terror, the panic, the fear—all had been present the instant she'd opened her eyes and gazed at the unfamiliar surroundings. And what had increased her agitation had been that she'd had no memory of getting to her present location.

Then the pounding in her eyes had taken over as she'd realised she'd fallen asleep with her contacts in. Trying to get out of the bed, her feet had become tangled in the blanket, which had been placed over her by...well, she presumed by Arthur, and she'd fallen from the bed, landing on the floor with a thud. The sound had only increased her own anxiety and she'd quickly removed the disposable lenses and looked around for a weapon. Her vision may have been fuzzy but the large book had felt solid in her hands.

At no point had she recollected coming to Arthur's apartment to feed Juzzy. At no point had she remembered closing her eyes as she'd sat on the floor with Juzzy on her lap, the two of them snoozing together. At no point had she even contemplated she hadn't been somewhere safe because she'd been acting on instinct, on pure adrenaline. That had dissipated after she'd whacked Arthur with the book and he'd called her name.

Hearing him say her name—her *real* name—had been the only thing to break through her crazed thoughts. She'd instantly felt remorse for hurting him and embarrassment for having him see the side of her life she wanted to keep hidden. To his credit, he'd behaved in exactly the way she'd hoped he would, by listening to her talk and offering his support. He was quite a man.

Yes, she could have stayed tonight, she could have felt secure and comfortable in his arms, just as she had many times before, but what if she'd fallen asleep and woken up thrashing about? What if she'd hurt him again, hit him with an even harder object? And if she'd given in and stayed with him tonight, then she'd want to stay with him the next night and the next night and the one after that. If she was able to sleep soundly with him holding her, she'd never want to let him go.

Was that what he wanted? For her to become dependent on him? Was that what she wanted? Not only that, Arthur had come straight out and told her that he wasn't looking to do the marriage thing again. He'd been hurt once—and badly from the sound of it—and he wasn't about to embark on another adventure that might turn out to be just as disastrous. It was true that should she and Arthur start dating, there was no way in the world she would ever cheat on him. She most definitely believed in monogamy.

But Arthur had also told her that he wanted to focus on his career, on his research, and especially as he'd already obtained funding, which, in a highly competitive field, was a triumph in itself. The problem was that she had already lived a life where she'd often been considered second to a Petri dish. If Arthur really wanted to pursue that level of research, it would require all his attention and she didn't want to be in a relationship where once again she was playing second fiddle.

'Good things don't happen to you,' she told herself. 'Accept it as fact.' So it was a good thing she had left his apartment, that she'd hightailed it upstairs into her new sanctuary. Perhaps friendship was their only answer. There was too much water under the bridge for the two of them. They'd missed their opportunity and now the only avenue left open to them was that of very good friends.

Could she do that? Surely the weakness she felt in her knees every time he looked at her, or the way her heart raced whenever he smiled, or the tingles that enveloped her entire body when he spoke, would one day become a thing of the past? Right?

Maybelle sighed in exasperation and shifted on the lounge yet again, grudgingly agreeing Arthur had been right about the lounge needing some cushions. She needed pictures on the walls, too. She needed to put her own identity into this apartment. After all, she didn't have to move if she didn't want to.

She didn't have to move! The realisation was like being hit by a truck. The government had decreed the threat null and void. She was free and it wasn't until that moment that the truth of her situation started to sink in.

She'd told Arthur she wanted to find normalcy, to have a life like everyone else. She'd striven for years to find a level of normal but getting comfortable had often meant complacency and letting down her guard. Whenever she'd done that, bad things had happened. Being vigilant for so long had taken its toll on her but surely it wasn't going to stop her from really trying to make a go of a normal life.

Arthur had previously suggested taking her shopping for cushions and pictures and normal things, and as she glanced around the apartment she compared it to Arthur's. He had shelves filled with books, photographs on the mantelpiece and pictures on the walls. Yes, she had the necessities in life but it was sparse and bland. Would letting some colour into her life bring her happiness?

Was that really what her life was like? Sparse and bland? Would spending time with Arthur help her to get some colour into her world? She wanted to spend time with him, to be friends. Could they be just friends and avoid the frighteningly natural chemistry that existed between them from taking centre stage?

Rising from the lounge, she headed into the back bedroom, which still had several boxes waiting for her to unpack. She reached into one of them, pulling out various items until she found what she was looking for. Her old jewellery box. It was the one item she'd been adamant about holding onto, no matter how many times they moved. Carefully she opened it up, the tinny music starting to play.

She carried the box out to the lounge room and sat down, winding the box up when the music stopped. Inside the box, mixed in amongst her mother's jewellery, was something she had treasured ever since that night. She picked the item up and rubbed a finger over the face of the watch. Arthur's watch. The one she'd been timing him with when he'd been studying that night, the watch she'd put onto her wrist and then, when his father had come into the room and she had fled, it hadn't been until much later that she'd remembered she was still wearing it. As they'd been forced to leave their home that night, she'd kept the watch, secretly delighted she had something of his, something that could bind her to him.

If only things had turned out differently. If only…

When Arthur knocked on her door the next day, Maybelle was ready. They hadn't confirmed whether or not he was still taking her shopping but she was delighted he'd turned up. Earlier that morning she'd ignored the sensual dreams she'd had of him—the one where she'd woken with the memory of his kisses on her lips—and donned her armour of friendship. She was wearing denim jeans, running shoes, a T-shirt and an old baggy sweatshirt. If her hair had been long enough to pull back into pigtails she would have done that, but instead she fluffed the unruly curls and added a baseball cap. She was the exact opposite of sexy and the epitome of friendship.

'Wow. Don't you look like fun?'

Maybelle stared at Arthur with stunned surprise when those words came out of his mouth. What did she have to do to get him *not* to notice her? Wear a garbage bag?

'Fun?' She adjusted the hot pink baseball cap on her head and ran her finger around the rim of the brim. 'I'll have you know I take my shopping trips very seriously.'

'I stand corrected,' he remarked. He didn't venture into her apartment and instead waited on the threshold as though kept there by an invisible force field. Could he feel that tug? She could. Could he feel that spark that seemed to sizzle beneath the surface? She could. Could he stop glancing at her lips as though he wanted nothing more than to kiss her hello?

Maybelle jerked a thumb over her shoulder. 'I'll just grab my bag.' She walked off but called back to him, 'Are we taking your car?'

'Seems reasonable, given I know the way to the store.'

'Right. Right.' She returned with her bag and made sure she had her keys before closing the apartment door behind her. Arthur stepped back to allow her room but didn't venture towards the stairs. 'Something wrong?'

'You have the brown contacts in again.'

'Of course.' She walked towards the staircase, needing to keep things moving, needing to keep things on an even keel because when Arthur was around her, especially after the heat they'd generated together last night, she most definitely lost all focus—contacts or no contacts.

'Huh.' He followed her down the stairs. 'Short-sighted or long?'

'Short.' She cleared her throat as she reached for the front door to their apartment block. 'How's Juzzy this morning?' Maybelle was determined to keep the conversation nice and light, on general topics, and it seemed Arthur was only too willing to oblige. Perhaps he'd had second thoughts after what had happened last night? Perhaps he'd regretted telling her what it was he wanted out of life? Perhaps he, too, thought it was wise to put some emotional distance between them?

As he chatted about the dog's antics that morning, Maybelle took the time to peruse him more thoroughly. He, too, was dressed comfortably in a dark pair of denims and a black jumper. Casual but not dressy. He could walk into a casino or a fast-food restaurant and seem completely at ease in both. He looked good, though, really good, and she bit her lip in an effort to distract her mind from the memories that were starting to rise to the surface.

Arthur drove to the district where several homeware and furniture stores were located. Maybelle couldn't believe how different the area was from when she'd lived here. 'So much has changed,' she murmured, not realising she'd spoken out loud until Arthur chuckled.

'What did you expect? Twenty years is a long time, Maybelle. Progress does tend to happen.'

'Oh, no, look. There. That restaurant. I remember that restaurant. It was an Italian restaurant with awesome food.'

'Still is.'

'Ha! Something stayed the same.' She sighed with happiness, then glared at Arthur when he laughed at her again. 'What's so funny?'

'You. You're such a juxtaposition unto yourself.'

Maybelle rolled her eyes. 'Whatever, mate. I just know what I know and like what I like and you can take that anyway *you* like.'

'That type of attitude should make picking houseware a real treat. Next you'll tell me that you're not really sure what you want but when you see it, you'll know.'

'You know me too well.' They were the wrong words to say as it brought back just how well he did know her. She glanced at him and he glanced at her, before they both returned their gazes to the front windscreen.

'Let's have some music.' Arthur quickly turned on the radio, needing to break the awkward tension that was starting to swirl around them. Thankfully, it wasn't too much longer before they arrived at the store and when they entered, Maybelle clasped her hands tightly together. Not because she was excited to be here but because there were just so many people around.

The store was huge, a wide open-plan store that was set out in departments. There were dining-room tables and chairs on one side and sofas on the other. In the far right corner were beds of all shapes and sizes and to the left was a different section, which had pillows, curtains and household linen.

In the rear part of the store was another large area where she could see kitchen appliances, cameras and computers. Streamers and balloons were everywhere, brightly coloured and moving slightly with the breeze from the heaters, which were working overtime trying to keep the people in the store warm against the outside weather.

Parents, children, babies, prams, pregnant ladies, pensioners and couples of all ages seemed to have congregated in this one large store all at the same time. The sales staff were easily distinguished in bright red blazers and several were walking the floor, offering their assistance to the patrons.

The noise. The heat. The lights. The decorations. Everything blurred into one big headache and Maybelle breathed out slowly in order to try and calm her rising panic.

'Are you all right?'

She looked at Arthur, surprised to see a worried look on his face. 'Why?'

'Because every muscle in your body is tense. Your jaw is clenched. You're squeezing your fingers so tightly together, your knuckles are turning white. What is it?'

'It's nothing.'

'Rubbish.' He placed a hand beneath her elbow and steered her carefully to the corner of the store, where he sat her down on a small sofa. Arthur sat next to her and placed a hand over hers. 'Tell me what's happening, Maybelle. Let me help you. Please?'

'It's just very…busy.'

'In the store? Do you want to leave?'

Maybelle stopped looking around at everything and focused her attention on Arthur. He was concerned. She could see it in his eyes and hear it in his voice. He was concerned...for her. How was she supposed to resist him when he cared about her so much?

'Talk to me, Maybelle. Don't shut me out. Tell me what's going through your head. Let me help you find that new normal you're so desperately seeking.'

She dragged in a breath, held it for a moment, and then slowly exhaled. 'Large places like this,' she began quietly, 'can be dangerous. When you're trying to hide from someone, they're good. You can blend in with the crowd but at the same time it means there are more people around to keep your eye on, to ensure you don't accidentally bump into the person you're trying to get away from.'

Arthur slowly shook his head, compassion and concern etched in his expression. He didn't say anything but his thumb was rubbing her hand gently, as though urging her to continue.

'The instant we entered this building I scanned the place for the exits. I do it everywhere I go. It's become part of my normal routine. In here, apart from the main doors where we came in, there are eight. Some are normal entry and exit ways, but the others—over there behind the linen department and the one next to the kitchen appliances—are for the staff and no doubt lead to the stockrooms. There are thirteen desks where people can sit with staff and discuss their purchases and in the bedding section there's a small side room hidden behind the large plastic plant.'

'How did you do that?' Arthur turned his head to check out the areas she was mentioning, his jaw momentarily hanging open in surprise.

'When I was rescued after the first kidnapping, the government decided I needed some training in martial arts and espionage techniques. I didn't turn them down and the next time someone tried to kidnap me, that training kicked in. I had those kidnappers disarmed and on the ground with broken bones like a pro, then I escaped.'

'Uh…right.' She could hear the shock in Arthur's tone at her matter-of-fact words.

'That training has become ingrained. I can also tell you where the restrooms are, the disability ramps and how much this sofa costs. This is how my brain is wired. This is what I have to endure every time I walk into a new place. My mind seems to slip into covert mode and scans the room for possible threats and exits. I can't help it.'

'What about the hospital? The ED? Do you do the scanning thing every time you walk in?'

'Not so much now, but the first time, yes. The staff were captivated by some anecdote you were sharing.'

The side of his lips quirked upwards. 'I like to ensure we can laugh together. I find it helps the teamwork to be more cohesive.'

'That's the sign of a good leader.' She smiled at him and dragged in a calming breath, immediately feeling better. 'Thank you for listening.'

'Thank you for sharing. I know it must be difficult for you sometimes—'

'Like waking up in a strange bed and attacking you with a book?'

Arthur chuckled and rubbed his head. 'Certainly gets the adrenaline pumping.' He stared at her, the smile slowly fading from his lips. How was it that his eyes could change from joviality to seriousness within a split second? 'Whatever you need, Maybelle, I'm right here. Support, friendship, a shoulder to cry on.'

And she was right where she'd told herself not to be... gazing once more into Arthur's eyes and wanting him, so desperately, to kiss her.

CHAPTER NINE

'THIS ISN'T GOOD,' Arthur murmured, his words barely audible, but even if he hadn't spoken out loud, Maybelle was sure she would have heard him as the connection between them seemed to transcend the normal parameters of the world. Her heart was beating perfectly in time with his. How she knew this, she had no clue. She just knew. Their attraction was only magnifying their connection, their need for each other, and once again she had the urge to just go for it, to take their relationship to the ultimate consummation, and then she would have him out of her system. She could let go of the man who had been a large part of her world and she could move on.

He was looking at her lips as though he could kiss her with his caress and when she angled in closer to him, wanting the same thing, he slipped his arm further around her shoulders, gathering her near. When his gaze met hers once more, the fire, heat and desire was exactly what she'd been expecting to see...needing to see because she knew it matched her own.

'Why are we fighting this?' Again his words were so quiet but they reverberated loudly within Maybelle's heart and she placed a hand on his thigh and moved in even more, a hair's breadth from what it was they both so desperately wanted. 'I need you.'

'I know.' And with that, she pressed her mouth to his in the softest, most tantalising kiss she was sure they'd ever had. Such a feather-light touch, which caused a riot of fireworks to explode within her. Whether they were hot and hungry or as gentle as the beat of a butterfly's wings, the tension between them was always intense and she doubted that would ever change.

'I see the love seat is working its magic once again.'

The rude words were like a stylus scratching across the surface of an old vinyl record and they both turned to see a red-blazered sales assistant regarding them as though they were cute little cherubs. Her hands were clutched to her chest and the smile on her face was one of encouragement.

Arthur cleared his throat and eased away from Maybelle. 'Pardon?'

'The love seat.' The sales lady gestured to the sofa they were sitting on. 'We often have couples come and try it out. It's very comfortable and very…encompassing.' She spread her hands wide, then brought them together, her fingers linking as though to illustrate her point. 'Perfect for that wintry night, snuggled up by the heater, watching a movie.'

Feeling closed in with the woman hovering over them, Maybelle started to feel her earlier anxiety—the anxiety Arthur had been more than effective in quashing—begin to return. She didn't like feeling closed in, or patronised by pushy salespeople. Maybelle stood, pleased she was slightly taller than the other woman, and pulled her baseball cap down a little further. 'Excuse me.' She sidestepped the woman and walked towards the restrooms. She knew she was leaving Arthur to deal with the situation but he was more than capable of fending off a fawning piranha.

Her heart was pounding against her chest and she knew it was more from the way Arthur made her feel than anxiety. Chalk one up to sensual desire, she mused. A good cure for anxiety. In fact, she would be more than happy to have Arthur help her deal with her anxiety in such a way in the future and she knew he'd be willing to assist her with that research project. A small smile touched her lips and she felt her earlier dread begin to disappear.

She was doing normal things in the normal world. No one was here to kidnap her, there was no threat to her life any more. She would splash some water on her face, take five calming deep breaths, and go out and buy some throw pillows and pictures to brighten up her apartment. She could do this. She could.

Entering the restroom, she was immediately distracted by the sound of a woman in one of the stalls crying out in pain. Maybelle's professional persona was immediately on alert. She waited. Perhaps someone had a bad case of gastroenteritis. A moment later the sound came again.

'Are you all right?' Maybelle asked. The only reply she received was a panting and grunting sort of sound. 'Please? I'm a doctor. I can help.'

The next answer she received was another loud grunt, a cry and a yell all combined. 'I know that sound,' Maybelle muttered. She immediately bent down to check beneath the stalls, remembering seeing a heavily pregnant woman wandering around the store when they'd first entered and the woman had been heading towards the restrooms. 'Are you in labour? If so, are you able to unlock the stall so I can get to you?'

'Wasn't…supposed to be happening…yet,' a woman panted as Maybelle heard the sound of a locked latch being undone. She went into the cubicle, seeing a woman bending forward, half sitting, half trying to get off the toilet.

'How many weeks' gestation are you?' Maybelle asked

as she helped the woman to manoeuvre out of the stall and onto the floor of the bathroom.

'Twenty-eight.'

Maybelle was surprised as the woman looked much bigger. 'Twins?'

'Yes. Girls.'

'I'm Maybelle, by the way,' she said as she pulled her cellphone from her pocket and called Arthur.

'Jenna.' She slowly let out a long breath, then leaned back against the wall as the contraction passed. 'I think it's all right now.'

'I disagree,' Maybelle replied, then turned her attention to the phone as Arthur answered. 'Can you come into the women's bathroom, please? I have a woman in labour.'

'Who are you calling?' Jenna demanded as Maybelle disconnected the call.

'The director of the emergency department at Victory Hospital. He's right outside.' She smiled at Jenna.

'Are you an obstetrician?'

'No, we're both emergency specialists—and this most definitely classifies as an emergency.'

'I'd just said to Sean that something didn't feel right and that we should leave here and go to the hospital but I needed to go to the—' Jenna stopped talking, wrinkled her nose and opened her mouth as another contraction started to make itself known. Jenna clearly wasn't backwards in letting her discomfort out, and as Arthur came into the bathroom he was greeted with a full-on yell of pain and anguish as only a woman in labour could make.

'You weren't kidding.'

'Is there a first-aid kit nearby? And can you get some towels or sheets or both so I can at least make a steril-ised area?'

'Being in a store that sells all those things shouldn't

make that request too difficult,' he replied, and headed out again. Maybelle stood and took off her hat before thoroughly washing her hands, coaching Jenna through her breathing. When the contraction started to subside, Jenna tried to lever herself from the floor.

'What are you doing?' Maybelle asked as she finished drying her hands with the hand-dryer.

'I'm standing up.' Jenna glared at her as though she was insane. 'I need to get to hospital and get this labour stopped. My girls aren't done yet. I still have twelve weeks left of my pregnancy and—' Jenna's words were cut short as her abdomen contracted once more and she immediately slumped back against the wall, wrinkling her nose and crying out in pain.

'That was less than a minute between the two contractions,' Maybelle stated as she knelt down, being careful not to touch her hands against anything. 'Jenna. I need to check to see how far dilated you are.' The woman's underwear was still around her ankles and her shoes had somehow come off but thankfully she was wearing a skirt, which Maybelle lifted up with her elbows. As Jenna continued with the contraction, concentrating on her breathing but screaming in pain every now and then, Maybelle was extremely surprised to see a tiny hand presenting first—as though waving hello and letting everyone know that no matter how much they may wish to stop this labour, it wasn't going to happen.

'Your waters must have broken because things are definitely progressing fast,' Maybelle told her just as Arthur came back into the room with a first-aid kit. Behind him was the store manager, carrying a bundle of fresh towels and sheets, along with a pillow and blanket for the labouring woman, which he quickly placed on the floor and then rushed out, telling them he would ensure they had privacy.

As Maybelle pulled on a pair of gloves, Arthur pulled the clean sheets from the packets and spread them around the area where Jenna now slouched.

'I found some paper straws, which we can use in place of suction, and also some bag clips to clamp the cord if the ambulance doesn't get here in time.'

'It won't,' she told him softly, and indicated the little hand.

'Ah...'

'Scissors?'

'Should be some in the first-aid kit.'

'Good.' Maybelle nodded and went back to coaching Jenna as the contraction started to ease once more. This time Jenna didn't even bother to move, except when Arthur needed her to lift her bottom so they could get the clean sheet and a comfortable towel beneath her.

'And look...the sheets are nice and pink. Perfect for two little girls.'

'Ambulances are on their way.'

'Ambulances? More than one?' Jenna asked, a little dazed and light-headed. Before Arthur could answer, there was a ruckus at the closed bathroom door with raised male voices.

'I'm sorry, sir,' came the store manager's voice. 'There's an emergency in progress.'

'Where's my wife? My wife was in there! She's pregnant. Jenna! Jenna?'

'Sean?' Jenna called back, and within the next moment a man came bursting into the women's restroom and rushed over to his wife's side. 'Where were you?' She burst into tears as he crouched down by her head and hugged her close, kissing her.

'I was still looking at the cribs. I'm here now.'

'So are our girls,' Jenna managed to get out as another

contraction came. Maybelle supported the little hand, which was up beside the baby's head, as she talked Jenna through the contraction. Sean's eyes widened as he looked at what was happening.

'Is that a hand?'

'Yes,' Arthur answered. 'Sometimes babies are born with an arm above their head and given there are two babies in there, things may have been getting a little cramped.'

'Who are you?' Sean demanded.

'Shut up, Sean,' Jenna yelled between breaths.

'That's it. The head's almost out…now pant, Jenna. Pant. I just need to check that the cord isn't around the baby's neck.' Maybelle's tone was calm and controlled, as were her actions as she confirmed the tiny little neck was clear of the cord. 'Arthur?'

'Ready,' he told her.

'OK, Jenna. With the next contraction, I want you to focus all your energy on pushing down. That's it. Good. Good. Grit your teeth and… That's it! Baby girl number one is out.'

Maybelle expertly handled the tiny twenty-eight-week-old baby and held her out so Arthur could wrap her in a towel. The fluffy new towel almost engulfed the baby, which Maybelle guessed to be less than one kilogram in weight.

Arthur was rubbing the baby with the towel, trying to stimulate blood flow and breathing. Maybelle grabbed the box of paper straws Arthur had brought in and pulled one out, sucking the mucus and gunk from the baby's mouth then nose, spitting the contents onto the sheet surrounding the area.

'Why isn't she crying?' Jenna's voice was tremulous, worried and extremely concerned.

'They're working on it,' Sean soothed, as he watched what was going on. Once Maybelle had finished sucking out the nose, the little one dragged in a fighting breath, gasping a little as Arthur continued to rub the vernix off and stimulate blood flow.

'New towel,' he stated, and Maybelle reached for another one and accepted the baby from him.

'Nostrils are flaring a bit and there's sternal recession.'

'Wh-what does that mean?' Jenna's tone was almost hysterical and with good reason.

'Baby's having a bit of trouble breathing,' Maybelle told the new parents. 'But she's a fighter.' Maybelle was about to pass Arthur two of the bag clamps so they could clamp off and then cut the umbilical cord when Jenna's body tensed with another contraction and she started to yell once more from the pain.

'Give me the one-minute Apgar,' Maybelle told him as she returned her attention to delivering the next baby. Arthur was more than capable of clamping and cutting the cord. Ordinarily, they'd get the father to do it but right now there was no time for formalities. These little girls needed expert attention and it was up to them to provide it. 'All right, Jenna. Here we go again.'

'Isn't the ambulance here yet?' she panted as she tried to breathe her way through the pain racking her body.

'One-minute Apgar is six and a half,' Arthur stated and Maybelle nodded.

'You're doing great, Jenna. Let's just focus on what's going on here. I can see the baby's head. It's bigger than the other twin.' She paused and checked, feeling around. 'Quite a bit bigger.' Maybelle glanced over at Arthur, her look indicating that something wasn't completely right with this whole situation. It would be wonderful if they had a baby heart monitor, or a stethoscope or even an old

Pinard horn so she could check the other baby's heart rate because what she was thinking meant that the baby who was still to be born wasn't about to have an easy ride.

'When was your last check-up?' she asked Jenna as the contraction eased. Jenna closed her eyes and rested her head against her husband's shoulder. 'Sean?' Jenna needed to rest and if she didn't feel up to answering questions then her husband could do it for her. 'When was the last check-up?'

'Last week. Our obstetrician wanted Jenna to have a scan on Monday because she had some concerns.'

'Did she happen to say what those concerns might be?'

'She told us one baby was bigger than the other but that it should settle down. She wanted it monitored closely, though. Why? What's wrong? Is there something wrong with our little girls?'

'Sean!' Jenna growled at him. 'You're freaking me out. Just let me get through this delivery.'

'This next baby is quite a bit bigger than the other.' Maybelle spoke softly to ensure Jenna remained calm and focused.

'That's OK, right? Our doctor said that neither of the twins were the same size as a normal baby…you know… if we weren't having twins.'

'Yes, that's right, but one big twin and one small twin can sometimes mean one has been greedier than the other in the womb.'

'Fighting already?' Jenna groaned, before gritting her teeth as another contraction began. Once more, Maybelle looked at Arthur and he nodded as though he received the silent message she was sending.

'Are the babies identical?' Arthur asked as he continued to care for the tiny baby rugged up in the fresh towel.

'Yes. They share a placenta.' Sean answered immediately, proud that he knew and understood that much.

'Oh. Did your doctor talk to you about the possibility of twin-to-twin transfusion?'

'She said a lot of things,' Sean answered when Jenna seemed more focused on getting the job done, rather than answering questions. As Jenna started to push, Maybelle focused her attention on delivering the baby's head and while this one was bigger than the first twin, it was still quite tiny compared to a baby carried to full gestation. 'Just checking there is no cord around the neck...and we're good. Excellent panting, Jenna. Almost there. Almost there now.'

The store manager opened the door for a moment and announced that the ambulances were pulling into the car park.

'There you go. Good news. Keep pushing, keep pushing,' Maybelle encouraged as Jenna continued to deliver her second daughter. Arthur announced the five-minute Apgar for the first baby to be eight.

'Good,' was Maybelle's reply.

'Sean. I need you to come and hold your daughter,' Arthur told him, and beckoned him over. 'Open your shirt and we'll put her on your chest.'

'My chest?' Sean's eyes were already wide at what was happening but they grew even wider at this.

'Body heat. It's the best way to keep her warm.'

The bemused Sean opened his shirt and Arthur placed the baby on his chest. 'Hold her firmly and watch her in the mirror—that way you can report any breathing difficulties or change of colour. It's imperative we keep her warm. See how she's breathing a bit better than she was before? Now you need to keep her in this position. We need to be able to see her breathing. See her sternal area?' Arthur indicated the area where the baby's chest was rising and falling as she breathed. 'Keep her at this angle because it helps get air into her lungs. We also need to make sure we support her head and not move her around too much.'

'Are you sure I should be holding her?' Sean asked, clearly freaked out by holding his extremely tiny baby girl.

'Yes. I need to help with your other daughter and, as you're her father, who better qualified?'

'Father!' Sean's eyes suddenly registered the truth of the word.

Arthur smiled but left the tiny baby girl in her father's more than capable arms before preparing to accept the second daughter from Maybelle. Towels at the ready, it wasn't long before the little girl was out of the womb and into his waiting hands.

He wrapped her up and started to stimulate the blood flow, the poor little thing grunting for air. Maybelle used the straws once again to suck out as much mucus and gunk as she could from the mouth then the nose, in order to clear the airways, but still the baby grunted, the breaths shallow.

'What's happening?' Jenna asked as she lay back, eyes closed, but the concern in her tone was evident.

'This one's having difficulty breathing.'

'But she's really red and a good colour,' Sean interjected.

'She's too red,' Maybelle said as she readied another towel after Arthur had finished wiping all the vernix off. 'What are you going to call the girls?' She pressed her fingers to the baby's umbilical cord in order to take a pulse.

'The first one is Poppie and the other one is Lillie,' Jenna said, trying to open her eyes to see what was going on, but exhaustion was kicking in and they still had to deliver the placenta.

'Well, Lillie is red because she has too many blood cells.

It appears that although the girls were sharing a placenta, they weren't getting equal shares of the nutrients.'

'One-minute Apgar for Lillie is four.' Arthur continued to stimulate blood flow but they really needed to get her into the hospital and sort her out sooner rather than later.

'Is that bad?' Sean asked. 'Poppie's score was six and a half and—'

Before he could finish his sentence, the door to the restroom burst open and the paramedics came in, carrying their medical bags.

'Good timing,' Arthur said as they finished clamping and cutting Lillie's cord. 'Twin-to-twin transfer. Placenta still to be delivered,' he stated, as the paramedics knelt down to assist them. 'Maybelle, you and I need to get the girls to the hospital, *stat*.'

'The ambulance with the incubator is in the parking lot.'

'Excellent.'

'We'll take care of the mother,' the other paramedic told them as Maybelle and Arthur wrapped Lillie in another towel to keep her body temperature up. 'Oh, and by the way, the media's here. TV crew pulled up just after us.'

'Media!' Maybelle was the one who reacted and she quickly shook her head repeatedly. Not the media. She just couldn't deal with that. Not now. She'd already been emotionally exhausted from dealing with the crowds, fighting her attraction to Arthur and having to deliver sick babies! She'd been raised to keep herself hidden, to never appear on any sort of media, most of all on television.

'The store manager must have called them,' she heard someone say, but their words seemed far away, echoing around her. All she was conscious of was fear and panic beginning to grip her. The media…cameras…reporters… everything she'd been avoiding for years was right outside those doors. Her mouth went dry and her breathing increased as she tried to figure out a way she could escape without being photographed by any cameras.

'Someone clearly did,' Arthur replied as he handed Lillie to Maybelle, before retrieving Poppie from Sean. 'We'll take good care of your girls.' As she accepted the baby from him, she briefly met his gaze and tried to swallow over the dryness in her throat. Arthur's eyes widened imperceptibly as he recognised the panic in hers.

'Dr Maybelle here is going to give Lillie her undivided attention.' His words were pointed and Maybelle acknowledged them with a slight nod of her head. Yes. She had to concentrate on Lillie, on ensuring the little girl could breathe properly. Then Arthur picked up her baseball cap and placed it on her head, pulling it down so it obscured a lot of her face from the view of prying cameras. The action was so considerate, so nice, so thoughtful.

'They couldn't be in better hands,' the paramedic agreed, trying to fill both Jenna and Sean with confidence as their newborn twins were being taken away from them.

'Focus on the babies.' Arthur's words were warm and caring. He was standing just behind her, his warmth seeming to encompass her, calming her previously frazzled nerves. How was it possible that one reassuring look from him could instantly settle the anxiety she'd spent years trying to control?

'Because he's Arthur!' she whispered to Lillie as together they walked out of the store.

CHAPTER TEN

As they entered the ambulance, Arthur and Maybelle were solely focused on the babies.

'That wasn't so bad, was it?' Arthur asked softly as they placed the babies in a shared incubator. The paramedics shut the door, stopping the prying eyes of the media from watching them any further. As they'd exited the women's restroom and walked through the store, the media cameras had been rolling, reporters trying to ask them questions as they'd carried the babies through to the waiting ambulances. The store manager had been trying to clear a path for them, as well as getting himself in every photograph being taken, either by the media or others in the store.

Maybelle had kept her head down, focusing on Lillie's breathing, still stimulating blood flow, hoping it wouldn't take too long to settle down, but poor Lillie was still grunting and gasping for air.

'It went as well as could be expected,' Maybelle replied, as they made sure the babies were on their backs, their heads up. Thankfully, this ambulance was equipped for treating small babies and children. She found the smallest-sized mouth and nose mask in one of the drawers and attached it to the Laerdal bag before assisting Lillie with her breathing.

'Five-minute Apgar is around seven, which is a definite

improvement,' Arthur added a moment later after he'd attached an oximeter to Lillie. 'How's Poppie?'

'Oh, she's a fighter. Look at her colour. Nice and pink.'

They continued on to the hospital, their attention solely on the girls, and when they arrived, finally able to get some tests started for both girls, Maybelle checked Lillie's umbilical pulse and was pleased to find it improved.

They were met at the doors to the emergency department by one of the ED nurses and one of the neonate nurses.

'Twenty-eight weeks gestation monochorionic twins: Poppie and Lillie,' Maybelle stated, giving the staff the information they needed. 'Twin-to-twin transfusion with Lillie being the recipient, as you can see. Lillie's Apgar scores were four, then seven; Poppie's were six and a half, then eight.'

'Chest X-ray, cranial ultrasound, full blood count, blood gas and electrolyte levels,' Arthur added as they finished transferring the girls to their individual incubators. The nurses performed their observations and reported their findings.

'So tiny.' Maybelle checked Poppie's blood pressure reading, which was being monitored via the umbilical arterial line. She put her sterilised hand into the crib through the arm porthole and gently placed her hand on the girl's chest.

'Just as well we were out shopping.' Arthur's words were quiet as he visually assessed Lillie, the cardiac monitor letting them know her beats per minute had progressed to one hundred and ten. She was under the lights, the jaundice starting to appear.

Gemma came over to let them know that both Jenna and Sean were at the desk, wanting to see their girls. When Maybelle walked over to greet them, pleased that Jenna was in a wheelchair as she would be exhausted after her ordeal, she was astonished when Jenna grabbed her hands and pulled her down for a fierce hug.

'Thank you, thank you, thank you.' There were tears in the new mother's eyes. 'I hated it when you took my babies away but I knew you had to.'

Maybelle managed to murmur all the right responses as she slowly pulled back from the anxious woman.

'You saved my girls. You saved me. So many things could have gone wrong and yet—'

'We're not going to think about that,' Sean interjected as he placed both hands on the wheelchair handles and started to edge the chair forward.

'I was only in the maternity ward for a matter of minutes before they said it was OK to come and see our girls,' Jenna continued, as though Sean hadn't spoken, her desperation for her daughters mounting with each passing second. 'Can we see them? Can we?'

'Of course. They've both stabilised and we're getting ready to transfer them to the NICU.'

'What's that?' Sean asked, concern in his tone, and Maybelle smiled.

'Neonatal Intensive Care Unit. Let me introduce you to Iris. She's one of the NICU nurses.' Maybelle headed over to where Lillie and Poppie were lying, so tiny but so very much alive.

'Can we hold them?' Jenna's eyes greedily drank in the sight of her baby girls.

'Not for a few days but you can definitely touch them. No stroking, just putting your hand through to touch them.' Maybelle waited while they washed their hands, then took them over to their babies, the twins lying side by side in their incubators.

'What's wrong with Lillie?' Jenna shook her head as she

looked at her daughter hooked up to tubes and monitors. 'She's so much bigger than Poppie, but I thought Poppie would have been the one who was struggling.'

'In a twin-to-twin transfer, which is what's been happening here with your girls,' Arthur explained as he finished adjusting one of Lillie's monitors, 'Lillie's been getting the lion's share of the nutrients provided by their shared placenta. This means that Poppie has always been used to fighting.'

'You mentioned something like that when Lillie was born,' Sean added as he stared in wonder at his girls.

'Lillie, on the other hand,' Arthur continued, 'isn't used to fighting and hence why she's the one now needing more attention, but she's picking up. Her breathing has settled, her oxygen saturations are much better and her blood gases are improving.'

'They're improving.' Jenna sighed as she spoke, relief in her tone. Arthur and Maybelle stayed with Jenna and Sean until after the babies had been transferred to the NICU and once their obligations were done, they headed out of the hospital.

'That wasn't how I thought the day would go,' Maybelle commented as they walked towards the car park.

'Part and parcel of the job, eh?' he asked rhetorically.

'They're just so…tiny…so innocent. They have no idea how bad this world can be.'

'Or how good,' Arthur countered.

Maybelle glanced at him. 'There's more bad in this world than good, Arthur.'

'I beg to differ.'

'That's because all you've seen *are* the good bits. You got the good parents, the stable life, living in one house, doing the things that every normal person does.'

'And you got the bad,' Arthur stated. 'Not living in

one house, seeing the dark side of life and learning how to live in it, but, Maybelle...' He placed a hand on her arm to stop her movements and when she turned to face him, he spoke earnestly. 'You survived. You conquered. With everything that's been thrown at you, everything you've gone through, you won, honey. You won!'

'Did I?' She lifted the cap off her head and ran her free hand through her curls. 'I'm so confused, Arthur. Those twins...they've...confused me. They're so tiny and innocent and if I was their mother, I would want to wrap them in cotton wool and never let them out into the world.' She shook her head and returned the cap, needing the shield the brim provided. 'Why do people even *have* children? Why would they put them through the pain this world can bring?'

'Because, in normal circumstances, the good outweighs the bad.' Usually, she could keep her emotions under control and locked away but ever since Arthur had come back into her life, it was as though he'd brought her vulnerabilities out of the darkness and into the light. It was annoying because part of her wanted to keep everything locked away and hidden from sight, to keep her distance from Arthur and the dreams of a future together.

However, having seen those gorgeous little babies, so incredibly tiny and fighting for life with every breath, something deep inside Maybelle had burst forth and she found she *wanted* to tell Arthur about her past, to share her insecurities with him, to shine light on the darkness, because that was the only way it was going to disappear for ever. She now had firm images in her mind of what Arthur would look like holding a newborn babe and in her mind it was *their* newborn babe he was holding.

'Maybelle, you don't realise how gifted you are. Your trials and tribulations have given you such a unique per-

spective on all sorts of alternative medical situations. Take
Mr Bird, for example. If your life, your experiences had
been different, you wouldn't have even thought to check
the synthetic compounds in the anaesthetic.'

'Huh. I hadn't thought of it like that before.' She
frowned for a moment. 'I guess that can be said of all of
us working here. Our unique, personal experiences provide us with unique perspectives on the injuries and ail-
ments we treat in the ED.'

'Exactly.' Arthur smiled and couldn't help caressing
her cheek. 'You're unique, Maybelle, in *so* many ways,
and regardless of what happens in your future, whether
you have children…' his voice dipped slightly at the word
and his gaze momentarily encompassed her lips '…or not,
you'll still be able to bring your unique perspective to everything you do.' He shifted closer to her, his gaze flicking
between her mouth and her eyes, the tension surrounding
them beginning to thicken with repressed desire and need.
'For the record, I think you'd make an incredible mother.
Fierce and protective but still able to enjoy those moments
of pure happiness.'

'Do you think so?' The uncertainty in her voice was
his undoing and he began to lower his head towards hers.

'I have no doubt.' His words barely a whisper, he
brushed his lips across hers in one of those insides-melt-
ing, heart-thumping, teasing butterfly kisses.

'Arthur?'

'Yes, honey?'

'You confuse me more than anyone else.'

'How so?'

'Because I…I…' She stopped, biting her tongue. She
was exposing herself, making herself vulnerable. They
were in a public place, anyone could see them kissing,

whispering, staring at each other with pure lust and desire in their eyes.

'I really want to be friends with you, Maybelle,' he remarked softly. 'I keep telling myself that over and over but then you look at me and I get all twisted up inside.'

'I'm sorry.'

'No. Do not apologise. I like getting twisted up by you.' He ventured another butterfly kiss and she almost melted into his arms, momentarily not caring who saw them. 'Is this thing we both clearly feel a residual from all those years ago? That because our relationship was cut short—'

'We never got to see how it really ends?' she asked, finishing his sentence.

'There has never been anyone who has made me feel the way you do.'

'Not even your ex-wife?'

'No. Only you make me this crazy, this determined, this afraid.'

'Afraid? You're afraid of me? I promise I won't slug you with any books ever again.'

He chuckled and shook his head slowly from side to side, caressing her cheek before dropping his hand and stepping back. 'That's not what I meant. I mean…how I feel about you, how I feel when I'm with you, how I feel when I'm without you.'

She nodded. 'Me, too. That's exactly how I feel. I'm confused and I'm happy and I'm scared and…and I don't know which way is up.'

'Then…' He paused for a moment and exhaled slowly. 'What if we…cautiously…research this attraction? Instead of trying to deny it, we explore it.'

'To see if it *is* just residual?'

'Exactly.'

'And what if it is? What if we try this and it fizzles out?'

'Then we can go back to being friends because that's the one part I don't want to lose. I don't want to lose your friendship, Maybelle.'

'So we do some *research* into exactly what this is we're both feeling.' Even saying the word 'research' made her feel nauseous. She gritted her teeth and momentarily closed her eyes. It was just a word…a word, that was all, and yet it made her stomach churn.

'What's wrong?' he asked cautiously when she looked at him again.

'Nothing.' He fixed her with a look that indicated he knew she wasn't being completely honest with him. 'It's just that…' She felt stupid even telling him this.

'What?'

'The word *research*—it…it makes my stomach churn.'

'But it's just a word.'

And now he was looking at her as though she was insane. 'Don't you think I know that and I also know that not all…scientific investigations…' she paused, using the alternative for the word '…are bad? And in this case, it's only right that we figure out what it is we feel for each other.'

'But hearing the actual word makes you feel ill?'

'Yes.'

'However, you're willing to do some…scientific investigation into how we feel about each other?'

She nodded, pleased he'd listened to her. Even if he hadn't completely comprehended what it was she was saying, it was nice of him to avoid the word on her account. She relaxed for a split second before tensing her shoulders once more as a new thought occurred to her. 'But wait a second, what if one of us feels it's great and the other one doesn't?'

Arthur frowned. 'Huh. I hadn't thought that far. I'd always assumed we'd both be unanimous in our decision.'

'Something still to consider, then.'

'Yes.' His frown deepened. 'Should we go for it, then? Embark upon this new re— Er...new project?'

Maybelle considered it for a long moment. Research. Her parents had researched things together and apart but each time it had drawn them closer together. Perhaps that had been the formula all along where she and Arthur were concerned. They needed to do their investigations, to discover exactly what it was that existed between them, so she nodded. 'Yes. We embark on this new project.'

'OK.' The frown instantly disappeared, to be replaced by one of his glorious smiles. 'OK. This is good.'

'It is.' She smiled back at him, a slight awkwardness starting to surround them. 'So now what?'

'That's a good question.' He chuckled and the sound broke the tension. 'Dinner? Tonight?'

'Sounds great. Your place or mine?'

'How about we actually venture out to a restaurant? That Italian one we spotted earlier today.'

'A real date?' Why did the notion instantly fill her with dread? But, she rationalised, it was what normal people did. They would go out to dinner, enjoy a meal, talk and laugh and generally have a good time.

'Seems as good a place as any to begin our...investigation.'

'I'll pick you up at seven-thirty,' she offered.

Arthur leaned forward and pressed a kiss to her lips, sealing the deal. 'It's a date.'

When Arthur arrived home, he was still reeling from the fact he and Maybelle were actually going out on a date. Even all those years ago, they'd never been out on a real date so tonight would definitely be a first for them.

He couldn't believe how happy he felt, how right this felt, and with that realisation came a load of questions.

'All good research projects come with questions,' he told Juzzy as he fed her. 'Right? I mean, if we didn't ask questions, what would we research?'

The most prominent question was that after his disastrous marriage to Yvette he'd promised himself not to become embroiled in a serious relationship again and here he was, not only embarking on a date but a date with the first girl he'd ever given his love to.

'She's not just any woman,' he told Juzzy. 'And that's what scares me.' She was an amazing woman, one who made him contemplate life in a different way, one who challenged him at work to research further and look deeper into patient problems, one who made his heart miss a beat every time she smiled at him.

He walked into his bedroom and reached far back on the top shelf of his cupboard and pulled out an old shoe box. Inside were two photos of himself and Maybelle. One had been taken at her sixteenth birthday party before they'd kissed. He had his arm around her in a brotherly sort of fashion and she was looking at him, smiling that secret smile of hers. Now, at least, he knew what that smile meant!

The other photo had been taken by Clara about five weeks later when the three of them had gone to Melbourne City for the day. There had been a parade on and both the girls had wanted to go. Arthur's mother had asked him to tag along to make sure the girls were safe. Arthur hadn't needed to be asked twice. This time they were sitting next to each other eating ice creams, both of them grinning brightly at the camera, and she had somehow managed to get ice cream on the end of her nose. She had been so carefree, so innocent back then. So different from the woman she was today…and he cared deeply for them both.

The other thing in the shoe box was a small pink pen with a top. She'd used that pen on the last night they'd had together, writing *Arthur smells delicious* on his revision notes. He'd thrown the piece of paper out after she'd vanished from his life, but for some silly reason he'd kept the pen.

He took the box out to the lounge room as his cellphone rang. He immediately hoped it wasn't Maybelle calling to cancel their date but rather that she was calling to say she wanted to start the date earlier…as in right *now*. But it wasn't Maybelle, it was his sister.

'Hey, sis,' he said after connecting the call.

'Hey, bro,' she returned, following through on the usual way they greeted each other over the phone.

'What's happening?'

'I could ask you the same question.' There was a tone to Clara's voice that made him wary.

'What are you talking about?'

'Maybelle Freebourne? The woman you haven't been able to stop mentioning in your emails and text messages? Remember her?'

'Sure. What about her?' Did Clara know? He hadn't said anything about Maybelle's true identity to his sister simply because it wasn't his secret to tell. Until Maybelle told him that Clara knew, he had to keep silent.

'Do you remember what you wrote in your last email? About how you like spending time with her and that she makes you laugh and how Juzzy thinks she's amazing?'

'Juzzy *does* think Maybelle is amazing.' He sank down into the lounge and stared at the pictures on his mantelpiece, especially the one with Clara and Maybelle at their birthday party.

'Are you crazy? You're falling in love with this woman!'

Clara had a valid point, although Arthur had to wonder whether he'd ever really fallen out of love with Maybelle.

'Why would it be crazy if I was in love with someone?'

'Because of what Yvette did to you! Because of what Virgil did to me! We made a pact, remember? We said we'd give up on love and focus on our careers and then that way we'd spare ourselves from ever feeling as though our lives were worthless, meaningless and downright depressing.'

He sighed. 'We did say that, didn't we?'

'On your last visit to see me.' Clara sounded crushed.

'I'm sorry, sis. I'm sorry Virgil broke your heart but at the moment I'm not sorry that Yvette broke mine.'

'What? How can you say that? She cheated on you with any man who looked twice at her and then blamed you for not being progressive enough to want an "open marriage".'

'If Yvette hadn't broken my heart, it never would have mended again.'

Clara paused. 'You really are in love with this Maybelle Freebourne woman, aren't you?' His sister's tone was softer now, more calm.

'I don't know for sure but one thing I have realised is that I need to try. If she breaks my heart, *then* I'll give up on love for ever.'

'Promise?'

Arthur chuckled. 'Promise.'

'Well, I'm now really looking forward to meeting this woman in four weeks' time.'

'Four weeks, eh? You're coming home? For real this time?'

'Yes. For real this time. I've booked my flight and I'll send you the details so you can pick me up from the airport.'

'Oh, thanks.' While Clara talked about her plans for the next month, Arthur kept a close eye on the clock. Only four more hours until Maybelle was due to knock on his door…and he couldn't wait.

CHAPTER ELEVEN

WHEN MAYBELLE ARRIVED home from the hospital, she lay down on her bed, trying to get rid of the headache that had started not long after she'd suggested going on a real date with Arthur. Why should she be so concerned about it? Yes, they were going out to a public restaurant—something she hadn't done in…well, she couldn't remember the last time she'd gone out for a nice meal. Yes, she had trouble feeling so exposed in such a place but she had to keep reminding herself that the threat to her life was over, that she was free.

One of the last things her father had said to her before he'd passed away had been that he was sorry for her missed opportunities.

'I'm sorry you never got to date like a normal girl. That you never got to have your heart broken as a young woman because even getting your heart broken can build such strength of character.' He'd smiled at her, a small, sad smile that had pierced her soul. 'I'm sorry you never get to go out to dinner with a man, to have him send you flowers, to be courted in the way I courted your mother.'

'Dad, it's not as though I haven't dated over the years—' She'd tried to interject but her father had hushed her.

'I mean a real and long-lasting relationship,' he'd added. 'The kind your mother and I had.' Then he'd fallen silent for a long while, his eyes closed, his voice hoarse and barely audible. His breathing had been uneven and a few times Maybelle had checked his pulse to make sure he'd still been breathing. 'I'm sorry for everything we put you through but at the time we thought we were making a difference in the world, that we were making it a better place for you to live in, for our grandchildren and great-grandchildren.'

'So that's the main reason why you want me to find a fellow? You want grandchildren,' she'd teased, and had been rewarded with a small smile from her father.

'I love you, May, and I'm proud of you. Find someone. Find someone who loves you in the way you deserve to be loved. An unconditional love. A love that will stay with you for ever and never let you go, no matter what the consequences. Promise me.'

'I promise, Dad.' She'd spoken the words back then, promising him the world if she'd thought it would put his mind at ease. Now she spoke the words softly into the silence of her apartment. 'I promise, Dad, and I think I've found him. I think I found him long ago and I hope…I really hope that this works out because if it doesn't, well, perhaps I'll have to make do with living for my career, of making a difference in this world for future generations.'

At seven-thirty, Maybelle knocked on Arthur's door. Her hand was still raised when he opened it, as though he'd been standing on the other side, just waiting for her knock. 'Hi.'

'Hi.' He gazed at her, taking in the black trousers, red lace top with undershirt and big red coat. 'You look lovely.'

'So do you.' She appreciated his suit and chambray shirt. 'I wasn't quite sure what sort of attire the restaurant required so went with something I'd usually wear to work. Sorry.'

'Don't apologise.' Why were they both talking this way? So stilted? So formal? 'Uh…you ready to go?'

'Yes. Yes.' She stepped back from the threshold as he exited the apartment. 'Juzzy asleep?'

'She's eaten her dinner and is tucked up in her doggy bed.' He locked his door and then turned to face her. 'Would you like to take your car or mine? Because I'm more than happy to drive.'

'I'm fine to drive, too,' she stated, and then they both stood there, staring at each other for a long moment. Never before had Maybelle felt this uncomfortable with him. What was wrong with them? Now that they'd decided to actually pursue their relationship, to give it a try, were they both trying too hard?

When he didn't say anything else, she turned and headed towards the parking garage. Arthur followed behind and as soon as she drove out into the street, he turned the radio on. Discomfort reigned the entire journey to the restaurant and Maybelle kept trying to think of a decent topic of conversation that could keep them going for a while but her mind was too busy focusing on the uncomfortable tension.

It wasn't until they were seated in the restaurant, with large menus to hide behind, that Arthur cracked.

'This is ridiculous.' He put his menu onto the table and stared across at her. 'We shouldn't be this uncomfortable going out on our first date.'

'I think it's because we've both realised it *is* our first date that it *is* uncomfortable.'

'Then let's not call it a first date,' he ventured with a shrug. 'Let's call it a discussion, with food, about our… mutually beneficial scientific investigation.'

Even though he wasn't using the word *research*, which she appreciated, there was no other way to really disguise that what they were planning to embark on was, in fact, a research project. She sighed at the words.

'What's wrong?'

'It's nothing.' She looked at her menu. 'I think I'll have the gnocchi.'

'It's not "nothing". Tell me. What's wrong?' He reached across the table and touched her hand but the touch felt wrong, clinical and very...*researchy.* She tried not to recoil because deep down inside she really did want this to work. She wanted to be with Arthur. He was her knight in shining armour but right now he felt more like her lab partner.

'My parents were scientists.'

'I know.'

'Researchers.'

'I know.' He nodded, a small confused smile on his lips.

'They spent more time in their labs, studying the contents of microscope slides, mass-spectrometers and Petri dishes than they did with me.'

'I know.'

'As parents, they were married to their work, and as a child I could accept that.'

'What's your point?'

She shook her head. 'I don't want this...' she gestured to the invisible air between them '...to become an experiment. I don't want to be analysing every little thing, to be taking notes, comparing data.'

'I'm not saying that's exactly what we'll be doing.'

'But you said we should cautiously investigate the possibility of the attraction we feel.'

'Maybelle, what is it you're trying to say?'

'I don't know.' She closed her eyes for a moment and shook her head. 'Perhaps we're trying too hard. Perhaps coming out to dinner was a mistake.' She glanced around them, feeling highly exposed and self-conscious. 'I'm not good in open spaces. I'm not good at making small talk. I'm not good at these normal things.'

'You agreed to come to the restaurant. We could have stayed home.' He spread his arms wide.

'I know, Arthur. I'm trying to do the normal things but the more I try the more I realise that I'm not good at the normal things. I'm good at the abnormal things and—'

'May I take your order?'

At the sudden appearance of the white-aproned waiter Maybelle almost jumped through the roof, he'd startled her so much. Her knee hit the underneath of the table, causing the glassware to clink and the silverware to rattle. She had a fork clenched in her hand, ready to use it as a weapon if she needed to.

'I'm s-sorry...' the waiter stammered.

'You startled her,' Arthur remarked, smiling at the surprised man. At the same time Arthur leaned over and placed his hand over Maybelle's clenched fist, almost willing her to relax. 'Perhaps you could give us a few more minutes, please?'

'Of course, sir.' The waiter disappeared and Arthur tried to meet Maybelle's gaze. When he did, he realised she'd shut down. She wasn't going to open up and talk to him, not here, not now, not tonight.

'We can leave, if you'd like,' he said.

'We can?' She seemed surprised at that, unsure of the social parameters of dining in a restaurant. 'OK, then.' Without another word, she dropped the fork, collected her bag and coat, and walked quickly towards the door.

Arthur didn't want to delay too long in the restaurant, quickly apologising to the waiter and seating hostess, in case Maybelle left and drove home without him. On the drive back to their apartments she was silent. It wasn't until she was at the foot of the stairs, ready to head up to her apartment, that she ventured to say anything.

'I'm sorry, Arthur. I thought I could do this.'

'That's OK. Perhaps we should have eaten at home, at least until you get the hang of being out in public spaces and—'

'I meant you and I. I thought I could do this—that I could be impartial, try to see whether the feelings we have are residual or something more…but I can't.' She started up the stairs.

'Maybelle, wait. It's just a trial run. Remember we'd agreed that if we both feel it isn't going to work, we'll go back to being just friends.'

'I'm sorry, Arthur. I can't do this.' She continued up the stairs.

'That seems to be your answer for anything you don't like, Maybelle,' he called. '"I can't do this". Well, I have a question for you. What *can* you do? Huh? Let me tell you what you *can* do. You *can* tie a man up in knots and make him question his previous rational decisions. You *can* confuse a man so he doesn't know which way is up and you *can* break his heart if you continue to walk away.'

Maybelle tried not to listen, tried not to hear the pain in his voice, but his words pierced her heart. She leaned over the balcony and looked at him. '"I can't do this" means… I'm empty, Arthur. I have nothing to give you and the last thing I want to do is to infect you with my emptiness. All my life, every step and decision I've made has been analysed, first by my parents and then by the government. And the one time—the *one time* I allowed myself to throw caution to the wind, my mother died.' Maybelle choked back tears.

'I was held to ransom for two and a half days, locked

in a dark room with dirty water offered as my only means of sustenance, while my father went through the hell of being blackmailed. Finally, I was rescued with government operatives shooting dead my captors. I saw all that and once I was free I had to deal with the task of burying my mother. After that, I had to care for my father because he didn't know how to live without my mother.'

She shook her head. 'Relationships are hard. I know this and when I say I can't do this, I mean that I can't...' She stopped, her voice breaking along with her heart. 'I can't open myself up to you in case I lose you, too.

'The government's told me that the threat to my life is over but what if it isn't? That might just be paranoia talking but what if they come after me again, thinking I know the magic formula to give them their undetectable serum? What if they come after me...through you? I can't let that happen. I can't and I won't.'

With that, she turned and headed into her apartment, closing the door firmly on any relationship between herself and Arthur.

It was almost impossible for Maybelle to sleep at all that night, tossing and turning in her bed as visions of the life she'd always dreamed she'd have with Arthur floated around her. Part of her wanted to accept what he was offering with both hands, to run to him and wrap her arms around him and never let him go. The other part of her saw the two of them running from people who were chasing them in big black cars. Arthur was holding their daughter in his arms and she held their baby son as they ran.

Finally she managed to get them to safety, where they were no longer being followed, and Arthur looked at her with anger and hatred in his eyes, telling her this was all her fault, that he was taking the children from her so they could be kept safe. That he didn't want her or the trouble she'd brought into his life any more, that he didn't love her.

'Arthur! Arthur! No! No!'

Waking with a start, she sat bolt upright in bed, her face wet with tears. Her heart was thumping wildly against her chest as though she'd just run a marathon. It took a good five minutes for her to even move her head, her eyes still wide with fear as she looked at the clock. Four o'clock in the morning. That couldn't be right. She felt as though she hadn't slept at all. As she tried to untangle herself from the bedsheets, she realised she was covered in sweat.

It wasn't the terror of things that had happened to her that was causing her to feel so incredibly empty but the realisation that her life without Arthur would be worse than anything she had experienced.

'*I love him,*' she whispered as she walked slowly out to the kitchen, the coolness of the morning soothing her overwarm skin. 'I honestly love that man and I will never love another the way I love him.' Speaking the words out loud as she poured herself a glass of water only made her accept the depth of her feelings for Arthur. He was her other half. He was the man she'd measured all others against and she'd ruined it.

How she was supposed to keep working alongside him when she felt this way, she had no idea. She'd faced some difficult things in her life, hiding, changing her name, kidnappings, her mother's death and watching her father fade away to nothing. She'd been taught how to survive in a dark and sinister world but nothing had prepared her for the world of light and happiness. How was she supposed to survive?

Sitting on her lounge, she sipped the water and contemplated her dream. Bad things had happened and Arthur had blamed her. The look in his eyes, the look of hatred had been enough to scare her far more than anything else in her life ever had. She knew it had been a dream but dreams could come true, especially bad dreams.

Shaking her head, she tried hard to clear her thoughts, to push the panic of never having a life with Arthur out of her mind, and headed to the shower. She was up and awake, so she may as well get ready and head to the hospital. At least there she could bury her thoughts about Arthur in work…unless she saw him there…unless she was called to work alongside him.

'What am I going to do?' she wailed as she stepped beneath the water, the soothing droplets doing nothing to ease the tension in her shoulders. After her shower, she dressed and contemplated eating something, but when her stomach churned at the thought she grabbed her bag and keys and headed out the door.

She was halfway down the stairs when Arthur's front door opened. Reacting on instinct, Maybelle immediately turned and sprinted up the stairs back to her apartment, hoping he hadn't seen her.

'Maybelle?'

The sound of her name being called made her speed up, made her want to hide inside her apartment for the rest of her life. She managed to make it to the door but was fumbling for her keys when he took the stairs two at a time, coming to stand next to her just as she fitted the key into the lock.

'Maybelle, you can't start avoiding me.'

'Yes, I can.' She unlocked her door and went to go inside, but dropped her bag as she struggled to pull the key out of the lock. Arthur, being the incredible man he was, graciously stepped inside her open door, holding it for her while she picked up her bag and removed her key from the lock.

'Can't sleep either, eh?'

'I can sleep.' Her answer was defiant as she walked back into her apartment, knowing there was no way of avoiding him now. The conversation she didn't want to have was about to happen and she tried to steel her nerves by walking into the kitchen and switching the kettle on. Why couldn't they just go on living their separate lives, finding a sort of weird level of friendship so they could at least work together without things being awkward?

'I know you can sleep. I carried you to my spare bed, remember. You were *out* of it.'

Maybelle pointed her finger at him. 'Don't be cute.'

'That's a little difficult given my natural charm and charisma but for you…I'll try.' He leaned against the kitchen bench, watching as she moved around the kitchen. She wasn't sure what she was doing. She was trying to be busy, to make them tea or coffee or something, because she didn't want to talk about things, didn't want to face the truth of the situation.

'Maybelle.' He paused. She knew he was waiting for her to look at him but she couldn't. 'Honey—'

'Don't call me that.' Maybelle picked up the cloth and started wiping down the bench, completely avoiding the area where he stood. She was being a complete coward and that wasn't like her but when it came to facing the truth about how she felt about him, a coward she was. Putting the cloth aside, she clasped her hands together and turned her back to him. Closing her eyes, she counted to ten but still her heart continued to race and her brain refused to acknowledge any sort of rational thought apart from the tattooed rhythm of the words, *I love you. I love you, I love you.*

'Maybelle. I just have one question for you.'

'Hmm?' She opened her eyes and forced herself to look at him.

'Did you mean it when you said you couldn't lose me again?'

Maybelle thought for a moment, trying desperately to remember exactly what she'd said to him last night. She'd been distraught and over-emotional. Regardless, she knew the words were true. She would be devastated if something were to happen to Arthur, especially on her account.

'Yes.'

'And you can't enter into a relationship with me in case you let me down or hurt me, is that right?'

'Uh…' She went to pick up the cloth, to try and clean something again, but with her heart continuing to thump out that *I love you* tattoo, making her breathless with longing, wiping the bench seemed so incredibly meaningless. In fact, everything in life seemed incredibly meaningless…without Arthur. 'Uh…yes.' She nodded for emphasis.

'Oh, honey.' He took a step towards her and she immediately took one back. 'Will you just stand still for a second?' He took another step towards her and she remained where she was, her mouth dry, her knees turning to jelly and her every nerve ending in her body zinging to life as he slipped his hands around her waist. 'You're far more messed up in the head than I thought.' He brushed a kiss across her lips. 'But I love you, Maybelle. I don't think I've ever stopped loving you and I don't think I ever will. It's for ever, this love. For ever. I offer it to you, with all my heart and with no conditions. My love is yours. Unconditionally.'

'Unconditional love?' she breathed the words, unable to believe that what her father had told her to find, she'd actually succeeded in doing. 'You love me? *Really* love me?'

'I'll prove it to you.' Arthur drew her closer and pressed

his lips to hers. The way he kissed her, the way his lips held firm to hers for a long and powerful moment, the way he made her realise he wasn't going to let her go was also a promise. It was as though he was promising to always be there for her and Maybelle was having a difficult time wrapping her mind around that concept.

'But…' she managed when he eased back for a moment. 'But what about your career? Your research projects? You already have funding for one of them. That, combined with your work in the ED and running the ED and researching and career-ladder climbing and…when are you going to have time for a relationship?'

'I thought long and hard last night about everything you'd said, and I realised that what you were trying to say in the restaurant was that you didn't want to take second place to my work.'

'I spent all my life being way down the list of my parents' priorities.' Her voice was soft.

'I know, honey.'

'I can't live the rest of my adult life being way down on *your* priority list. I can't do it.' She shook her head as though to emphasise her words.

'You won't be. The re—the scientific investigation projects are each only six months in duration. Both of them will be conducted one day a week in the research laboratories attached to the hospital…and I'll be needing specialised staff to assist me with the investigations.' He looked deeply into her eyes. 'I know you've been through hell and all because of scientific research, honey, but the areas I'm looking into are *nothing* like the research your parents were conducting.'

'I know that. Don't you think I know that? Don't you think I know that not all research is bad? That the majority of research projects don't lead to life-threatening situations? The rational side of me understands that. However, the irrational side of me, the one that has been fed through surviving in such difficult circumstances…the side that makes my stomach churn at the mere thought of entering into any sort of research, tends to become predominant, causing me to behave like a crazy lady.'

He couldn't help but chuckle softly at her words. 'You might be a crazy lady, honey, but you're *my* crazy lady.'

'I am?' He clearly wasn't put off by what she was saying and that astonished and delighted her.

'You're also the smartest girl I know. I told you that years ago and it hasn't changed now, which is why I would be honoured if, for that one day a week at the hospital labs, you'll work alongside me, taking part in the scientific investigation and applying your incredible intelligence to it.' He brushed his hand across her cheek, gazing into her eyes. 'I want you near me. I want you with me…all the time. I lost you for twenty years and I couldn't possibly put anything in my life first…except you. I was in a marriage where I was most definitely not first in her eyes, and when that marriage ended I told myself it was easier to be married to my career. My career wouldn't let me down, it would always be there. There's always re—scientific investigations that need doing. But then you came back into my life and… Maybelle, honey, you changed everything. *Everything*. Yes, I want to help people by being a doctor but if I had to choose to be with you or to practise medicine, I'd choose you.'

'I don't want you to choose. I want to—'

He pressed his finger to her lips to silence her. 'I know you're not asking me to choose. I know you respect my work, not only as a doctor but as an emergency specialist. You get that and I know, once you read my research proposals, you'll become as passionate about the projects as I am…because I know you. You give and you give and you give, and again that's just another thing that I love about you.'

Tears had started to well in Maybelle's eyes at the way he was speaking so passionately, not only about her, and the way he thought she was intelligent, but about his work, and in that one moment Maybelle finally understood the relationship her parents had shared. It had been one of mutual love and respect but also an equal meeting of intelligence.

She couldn't help herself any longer and threw her arms around his neck and drew his head close to hers until her lips met his in a powerful kiss. She poured all her love into that kiss, and to let him know that she wanted to be with him, to share every aspect of his life.

'So you love me?' he asked a while later, and she was astonished to hear the slight hesitation in his tone.

'Yes. I do.' She felt rather than heard his sigh of relief.

'And I love you.' The words were spoken without hesitation.

'And we're going to work together at the hospital in the ED and in the labs…' She kissed him again.

'And on building a life together.'

Maybelle paused in her elation for a second as a thread of fear passed through her at his words. 'A life together… Arthur, what if…what if bad people *do* come after me again?' She shook her head. 'I had a terrible dream where they came after you and our children and…and…'

'I'll learn all the martial arts and protective measures and whatever else I need to, to ensure my family's safety,' he told her firmly.

'Family? Are you sure?'

He laughed and kissed her. 'Oh, Maybelle. You really are so perfect for me. I swore I'd never enter into marriage again but you were right. My heart wants to have a family, to have a house in the suburbs and to be with the woman I love for the rest of my life…and that woman is you.'

'Are you asking me to marry you?' She moved back and smiled at him.

'I believe I am. What do you say?'

She stood on tiptoe and kissed him before easing from his arms. 'I say, wait here a second.'

'That's not a yes!' he called after her as she rushed into her bedroom then quickly returned. She held out her hand and he opened his to accept whatever it was she was giving him. So trusting. She liked that.

Into his hand, she placed his watch. 'I've had this ever since that night. I've kept it safe. Kept it close. Kept it as a bond, linking us together.'

He shook his head with incredulity. 'You kept my watch.' He reached into the pocket of his trousers and pulled something out. He followed suit and held his hand out, waiting until she opened hers so he could place something on it.

'My pink pen? You kept my pink pen?'

'I think the ink's dried up, though.'

'You kept my pen.'

'You kept my watch.'

'We've stayed connected all these years.'

'It was meant to be.' He drew her close once more.

'We belong together.'

'We do.'

'Marry me?'

'Yes.' Then she pressed her lips to his, hoping to convey her heartfelt love to the man who had always been her knight in shining armour…her King Arthur.

EPILOGUE

FOUR WEEKS LATER Clara Lewis arrived back in Australia
and was met at the airport by her big brother and his fian-
cée, Maybelle Freebourne.

'May! It's really you?'

Maybelle laughed as Clara completely ignored her
brother and embraced May as though the past twenty years
hadn't existed at all. Maybelle had had a similar reaction
from Arthur's parents, the Lewises welcoming her into
their family in the same way they had all those years ago.

Although Clara and Maybelle had spoken on the phone
several times during the past four weeks, seeing each other
face to face was very emotional.

She was glad Clara had returned to Australia when she
had, because in another three weeks Clara would be her
maid of honour, and Mr and Mrs Lewis would both walk
her down the aisle so Maybelle could marry Arthur and
officially become a member of the Lewis family.

'It's what I'd always hoped,' Clara whispered in Maybelle's ear as they continued their hug. 'You're really going
to be my sister.'

'OK, you two. Break it up,' Arthur remarked as he put
an arm around each of them, his beloved sister on one side
and his incredible future wife on the other.

'You're just jealous,' Clara sniffed.

'Completely. I've been used to having Maybelle all to myself. Now I have to share her and I don't like it one little bit.'

'Possessive, much?' Clara teased her brother as they headed off to the luggage carousel.

'Happy?' Arthur asked Maybelle later that evening as they sat on the lounge, Juzzy snuggled up between them.

'Beyond my wildest dreams. I've gone from being all alone to having parents, a sister and a dog.'

'What about me?'

'Oh, yeah. And an incredible man who loves me... unconditionally.'

* * * * *

*If you enjoyed this story, check out these
other great reads from Lucy Clark:*

*A FAMILY FOR CHLOE
ENGLISH ROSE IN THE OUTBACK
STILL MARRIED TO HER EX!
A CHILD TO BIND THEM*

All available now!

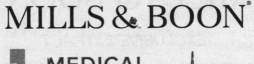

THE ULTIMATE IN ROMANTIC MEDICAL DRAMA

A sneak peek at next month's titles...

In stores from 29th June 2017:

Just can't wait?
Buy our books online before they hit the shops!
www.millsandboon.co.uk

Also available as eBooks.

MILLS & BOON®

EXCLUSIVE EXTRACT

Lana Haole and the all-too tempting Dr Andrew
Tremblay agreed to a marriage of convenience... But
suddenly their convenient arrangement has become a
whole lot more!

Read on for a sneak preview of
CONVENIENT MARRIAGE, SURPRISE TWINS

Lana's request had caught him off guard, but he wasn't
displeased by it. Not at all. It was just that he couldn't.
He'd just never expected it from her. She was always so
careful, guarded, but the more time he was spending with
her, the more he realized a hot fiery passion burned beneath
the surface.

And that was something he wanted to explore, but he
had a sneaking suspicion that if he tasted this once, he
was going to want more and more. So, even though it
killed him, he left the room. Walked the beach, far away
from the wedding, to calm his senses, but it didn't work
because all he could think about was Lana's lips pressed
against his.

The feeling of her in his arms.

And her begging him to make love to her.

You can't.

Although he wanted to.

After what seemed like an eternity he returned to the
room. Hoping that everything had blown over, that she
might be already asleep even, but instead he saw her sitting
on the couch, a flute of champagne in her hand. She turned
to look at him when he shut the door and he could see the
tearstains on her cheeks.

Pain hit him hard.

He'd hurt her.

"Oh, I didn't expect you to come back," she said quietly and she wiped the tears from her face.

"I just needed a moment to myself."

"I see," she said quietly. Then she sighed. "Well, I think I'm going to turn in."

"Lana, I think we need to talk," he said.

"What is there to talk about?" She frowned. "You didn't want me and you have nothing to apologize about. I'm the one that wanted to step out of the boundaries we set. Not you."

"No, that's not it."

"What do you mean?" she asked, confused.

"I want you too, Lana. It's not for lack of desiring you. I want you. More than anything." And, though he knew that he shouldn't, he closed the distance between them and kissed her, fully expecting her to pull back from him the way that he had pulled from her, but she didn't. Instead she melted into his arms and he knew that he was a lost man.

Don't miss
CONVENIENT MARRIAGE, SURPRISE TWINS
by Amy Ruttan

Available July 2017
www.millsandboon.co.uk

Join Britain's BIGGEST Romance Book Club

50% OFF your first parcel

- **EXCLUSIVE offers** every month
- **FREE delivery direc** to your door
- **NEVER MISS a title**
- **EARN Bonus Book** points

Call Customer Services
0844 844 1358*

or visit
millsandboon.co.uk/subscription

KCB3

MILLS & BOON®

Why shop at millsandboon.co.uk?

Each year, thousands of romance readers
find their perfect read at millsandboon.co.uk.
That's because we're passionate about
bringing you the very best romantic fiction.
Here are some of the advantages of
shopping at www.millsandboon.co.uk:

* **Get new books first**—you'll be able to buy
  your favourite books one month before they
  hit the shops

* **Get exclusive discounts**—you'll also be
  able to buy our specially created monthly
  collections, with up to 50% off the RRP

* **Find your favourite authors**—latest news,
  interviews and new releases for all your
  favourite authors and series on our website,
  plus ideas for what to try next

* **Join in**—once you've bought your favourite
  books, don't forget to register with us to rate,
  review and join in the discussions

Visit **www.millsandboon.co.uk**
for all this and more today!